The Sorrels of Savannah

The Sorrels of Savannah

Life on Madison Square and Beyond

Carla Ramsey Weeks

Table of Contents

The Sorrels of Savannah Family Tree

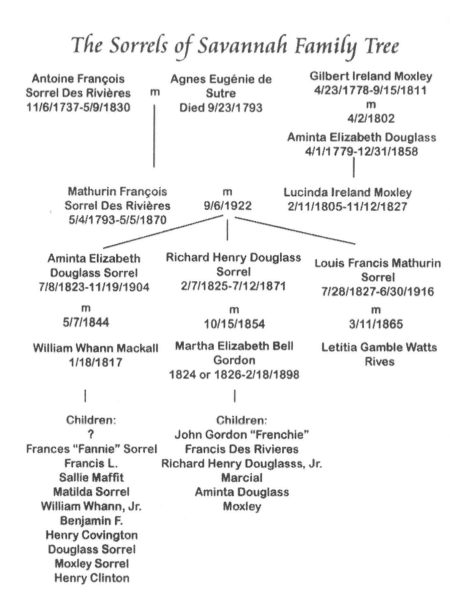

Antoine François Sorrel Des Rivières 11/6/1737-5/9/1830 — m — Agnes Eugénie de Sutre Died 9/23/1793

Gilbert Ireland Moxley 4/23/1778-9/15/1811 m 4/2/1802 Aminta Elizabeth Douglass 4/1/1779-12/31/1858

Mathurin François Sorrel Des Rivières 5/4/1793-5/5/1870 — m 9/6/1922 — Lucinda Ireland Moxley 2/11/1805-11/12/1827

Aminta Elizabeth Douglass Sorrel 7/8/1823-11/19/1904
m
5/7/1844
William Whann Mackall 1/18/1817

Richard Henry Douglass Sorrel 2/7/1825-7/12/1871
m
10/15/1854
Martha Elizabeth Bell Gordon 1824 or 1826-2/18/1898

Louis Francis Mathurin Sorrel 7/28/1827-6/30/1916
m
3/11/1865
Letitia Gamble Watts Rives

Children:
?
Frances "Fannie" Sorrel
Francis L.
Sallie Maffit
Matilda Sorrel
William Whann, Jr.
Benjamin F.
Henry Covington
Douglass Sorrel
Moxley Sorrel
Henry Clinton

Children:
John Gordon "Frenchie"
Francis Des Rivieres
Richard Henry Douglasss, Jr.
Marcial
Aminta Douglass
Moxley

The Sorrels of Savannah Family Tree, Cont.

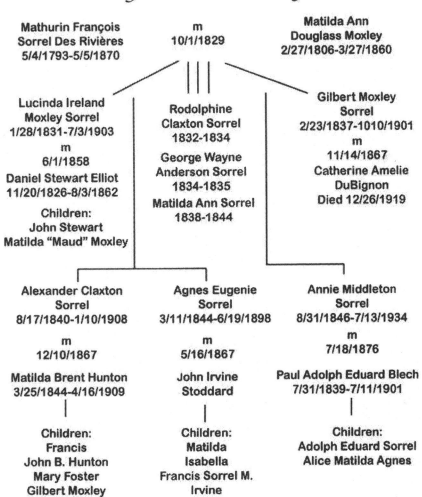

Mathurin François
Sorrel Des Rivières
5/4/1793-5/5/1870

m
10/1/1829

Matilda Ann
Douglass Moxley
2/27/1806-3/27/1860

Lucinda Ireland
Moxley Sorrel
1/28/1831-7/3/1903
m
6/1/1858
Daniel Stewart Elliot
11/20/1826-8/3/1862

Children:
John Stewart
Matilda "Maud" Moxley

Rodolphine
Claxton Sorrel
1832-1834

George Wayne
Anderson Sorrel
1834-1835

Matilda Ann Sorrel
1838-1844

Gilbert Moxley
Sorrel
2/23/1837-1010/1901
m
11/14/1867
Catherine Amelie
DuBignon
Died 12/26/1919

Alexander Claxton
Sorrel
8/17/1840-1/10/1908

m
12/10/1867

Matilda Brent Hunton
3/25/1844-4/16/1909

Children:
Francis
John B. Hunton
Mary Foster
Gilbert Moxley
Agnes

Agnes Eugenie
Sorrel
3/11/1844-6/19/1898

m
5/16/1867

John Irvine
Stoddard

Children:
Matilda
Isabella
Francis Sorrel M.
Irvine

Annie Middleton
Sorrel
8/31/1846-7/13/1934

m
7/18/1876

Paul Adolph Eduard Blech
7/31/1839-7/11/1901

Children:
Adolph Eduard Sorrel
Alice Matilda Agnes

Acknowledgments

In March of 2008 while on vacation in Savannah, my husband and I toured the Sorrel-Weed House at the invitation of owner Steven Bader. I was fascinated by the rich history of the house and the compelling story of Francis Sorrel and his family, first wife Lucinda Ireland Moxley and second wife Matilda Douglass Moxley, younger sister to the first, and their many children. The next day I returned to the house and talked with Steve about my interest in writing a novel based on the family who built his house. In order to write a novel based on the family, I wanted to know all that I could discover of the truth of the family. This history is the result of that quest.

Steven Bader jump-started my research by providing all that he had in books, documents, letters, and his personal collection of Savannah pictures. From there, I visited local and state libraries and archives, the Georgia Historical Society, and the Chatham County Courthouse, all of which provided gracious help.

In notes from Steve, I found the names of the Mackall brothers, Henry and Douglass, the great, great grandsons of Francis and Lucinda. They were wonderfully helpful, sending me all the information they had and the contact information for their cousins John Gordon and Jarvis Freymann, also great, great grandsons of Francis and Lucinda. It was with them that I really hit the jackpot. The Freymanns, along with their now deceased brother Moye, had done extensive family research and compiled the family photos that are used in this book. John Gordon has written a wonderfully informative and interesting paper, "The Sorrel Family in Saint-Domin gue (Haiti)," and it is from this paper that I have attained the information on Francis Sorrel's childhood, his father, and his French heritage. John Gordon and his wife Ruth also compiled a book for their children entitled *The Greatest Generation* in which they recorded all they knew of their great, great grandparents. This book, too, proved to be invaluable to me. John Gordon (Jeff) has done everything possible to help me find all I wanted to know by digging through everything he has, which is considerable, pointing me in the right direction when he didn't have it, and acting as a sounding board for speculation.

Thank you Steve Bader, Henry and Douglass Mackall, Jarvis and Jeff Freymann for making this book better than it would otherwise have been, and thank you, Jeff, specifically for your encouragement, your support, and your genuine enthusiasm. You've been a delight.

Too, I thank my mother and sisters for reading my work, offering their input, and supporting me always, Pammy Jo Andrews, my sister-of-the-heart, for her help with photography, and Ron, most of all, for making the research and writing of this history possible.

Introduction

The Sorrels of Savannah is a story of tragedy and triumph. They lived during tumultuous times in America's history. Francis built for himself and his family a lavish, privileged lifestyle in Savannah made possible, in part, by the institution of slavery. Their family was among the last generation of antebellum slaveholding southerners whose way of life was challenged and forever changed by the Civil War and Reconstruction that followed. The Sorrels of Savannah is an attempt to relate, in an interesting and readable form, all that I have gathered from Steve, the Mackalls, the Freymanns, and my own research and observations on this remarkable family. It is my desire and intent to preserve accurately and realistically the facts and stories of these historical characters while conveying their individual personalities and traits, both honorable and dishonorable, in a way that makes them real and merely human.

The Sorrels of Savannah—Francis, his two wives, and their children—are significant to history not just for their individual compelling stories, but that they offer a view of a family and their relationships with each other and the outside world during one of the most cataclysmic eras in American history. They give us a close-up, personal look of what life was really like for a relatively small but much publicized group of people: the slaveholding, white antebellum elite of Savannah, Georgia. Through their stories we are privy to life in the South before, during, and after the Civil War, and, best of all, we get unguarded glimpses of their personal lives and views through their interactions with each other during good times and bad. Through the unique lens of their individual personalities we are allowed to step back in time and hear their voices, know their thoughts, feel their fears, and witness their success and failure. I feel privileged to have experienced this journey back in time, and it is my hope that you too will feel a warm connection to and affection for the Sorrels of Savannah.

1

The Sorrels of St. Domingue

Antoine François Sorrel des Rivières

The story of Francis Sorrel and his family begins not in Savannah but in St. Domingue in the West Indies in what is now known as Haiti. It was there on May 5, 1793 that he was born to Antoine François Sorrel des Rivières and Eugénie de Sutré and named Mathurin François Sorrel. That Haitian-born child would grow up to be somewhat of an enigma, and in an effort to understand Francis, the boy he was and the man he was to become, one must look first at his parents, both of them mysterious characters in their own right.

John Gordon Freymann, in his paper "The Sorrel Family in Saint-Domingue" gives us the background of Antoine François Sorrel des Rivières, Freymann's great, great, great grandfather and the man who would become the father of Francis, the patriarch of the Sorrels of Savannah.

> *"Antoine François Sorrel des Rivières....was*
> *a scion of a prominent family in the Dauphiné,*
> *a province in southeastern France. The Sorrels*
> *had been country squires there since at least the*
> *early 15th century. More recently, some Sorrels*
> *had entered public service. Antoine's grandfather*
> *had been King's Counselor in Grenoble, and his*
> *father was....not only King's counselor but also*
> *Public Prosecutor and Comptroller-General of the*
> *Dauphiné."* (p. 2)

Antoine graduated from the School of Engineering at Grenoble, but because of a restless nature and an adventurous spirit, he was not content to follow in the footsteps of his father and his brothers who practiced law, entered the priesthood, or became landowners as had many generations of Sorrels before them. Graduating from the School of Engineering at Grenoble in 1757, Antoine went directly into military service. He longed to experience combat and did so in the Seven Years' War as a sub-lieutenant in the French Army. He was wounded not once, but twice. After his second injury, a serious chest wound from a bayonet thrust below the collar bone, Antoine was commissioned Geographic Engineer of Camps and Armies, a rank he held at the end of the Seven Years' War. Antoine was stationed in the port city of Brest where the Académie Royale de Marine was located, its responsibility being the coordination and improvement of French cartography. Freymann believes that he was probably attached to the Académie Royale de Marine after the war because of his specialty. ("The Sorrel Family in Saint-Domingue," p. 3)

The French were soundly defeated in the Seven Years' War, and at twenty-six years old, Antoine, a seasoned officer, was faced with career decisions. As a geographer-engineer, Antoine was a member of the best-paid branch of the French Army, and because his training made him valuable, he retained his salary after the war. The prospects for duty in Europe would have been unappealing to the adventurous Antoine as was a return to Grenoble and his father's way of life. Even though Antoine had probably inherited an estate from a relative of his mother, he wanted to seek his fortune outside his homeland. There was a tempting alternative—the colony of St. Domingue.

St. Dominigue was a French colony, but not just any colony. It was known as the "Pearl of the Antilles," the richest colony on earth due to its vast production of sugar, coffee, cotton and indigo. St Dominigue provided for a third of France's foreign trade even before its loss of Canada and Louisiana. France's losses in the Seven Years' War made the colony vital to their economic welfare. The economic center of the new world at that time, the colony exported forty percent of the world's sugar. Its plantation economy was driven by slave labor, so the black population outnumbered the white by eight to one. Most of the whites residing in St. Domingue were wealthy French colonists who traded their sugar directly with France.

Antoine may have been lured by the success of white, French colonists and the fact that geographer-engineers like himself were paid high salaries for colonial service. He knew that he, like many before him, could return to France a wealthy man, provided he could survive the yellow fever and malaria to which so many newcomers to the West Indies succumbed. Lt. Sorrel became a member of a delegation of men recruited in 1763 to map the interior of the islands. They probably reached the colony of St. Dominique sometime in 1764. Unfortunately, only a few of the party survived a yellow fever "seasoning period." Antoine was one of the lucky few.

Antoine not only survived in St. Domingue, he prospered. Six years after arriving in St. Domingue, Antoine married a young Creole heiress with a handsome dowry, quite an accomplishment since white men outnumbered white women about five to one. The term Creole was applied to anyone born in the colonies, regardless of their race. The heiress, seventeen- or eighteen-year-old Marie-Louise Perrine Augustine Ollivier du Petit Bois, owned four plantations in the region where Antoine worked as an engineer. Antoine and "Perrinette," as she was thought to be called, made the plantation at Miragoâne and a townhouse in Port-au-Prince their homes. Both of these residences were owned by Perrinette. The couple had three children, a son and two daughters. Antoine performed his engineering duties while living the life of a country gentleman. Records show that he was appointed Engineer-in-Chief of the Department of the West and royal general engineer in Port-au-Prince in 1782 and 1786.

One of the Antoine's daughters, Marie Louse François died at the age of eight, and his wife Perrinette died a few years later in 1786 at the age of thirty-three: both mother and child died in Port-au-Prince. Just five months after Perrinette's death, the governor of St. Domingue bestowed upon Antoine the commission and cross of a Chevalier of the Royal Military Order of St. Louis, the highest military Order of Chivalry extended as a reward for exceptional officers, an honor comparable to British knighthood. Antoine continued to prosper financially, as well, in St Dominique, so much so that he relinquished his equal share of the estate he had inherited in France to his three brothers.

Antoine and Perrinette's son, Antoine Auguste Théodat (called Théodat), and their daughter, Marie-Louise Antoinette Bonne (called Bonne), were both sent back to France to be educated. Antoine's father, also named Antoine Sorrel, was the boy's godfather. Théodat died in Port-au-Prince in 1802 at the age of 24 (family lore says he died in a duel). Bonne married Jean Marie Pinondel de Champarmois in September of 1795 but became mentally ill and lived out her life in a mental institution. It was her surviving husband that Antoine made his heir when he died.

By 1783, life in St. Dominique was still good for Antoine Sorrel. Though he had lost his wife and a daughter, he had remaining two healthy children; and thanks to Perrinette's wealth, he had the use of a plantation and a town house, the later in Port-au-Prince; and he had been knighted by King Louis XVI for his contributions to the colony. Antoine had accomplished what he had set out to do. He had become one of St. Dominique's wealthy elite. Little did he know that the way of life he had built for himself was about to change. The year 1789 brought the storming of the Bastille. The French Revolution had begun, and the "Pearl of the Antilles" was about to become a bloody battlefield.

The French revolution sparked conflicts among the castes of St. Dominique, the eventual result of which was an independent but devastated Haiti. Anarchy reigned in St. Dominique from 1789 to 1791 until the tens of thousands of slaves who had thus far continued to work their masters' estates turned on them with whatever weapons they could find. St. Dominique became an inferno as habitations were burned and hundreds of whites and mulattoes were massacred.

Antoine, as a knighted member of the Royal Army was, of course, loyal to King Louis, but in 1791 he encouraged a large group of *gens de couleur libres* (free people of color) to petition the governor of the colony for full civil and political rights. Antoine was apparently an ally of the mulattoes from the beginning of their campaign for equality, and this explains why Antoine survived the massacre of white officers and served with colored troops.

In the midst of social and political upheaval, Antoine had at some point married Eugénie de Sutre who would give birth to François in 1793. There is much mystery that surrounds François' mother, and probably with good reason. That period of history in St. Domingue was so tumultuous, it is little wonder that records are hard to find. In later years neither François nor his father Antoine were willing to talk about Eugénie de Sutre. François never knew his mother. She died only seven weeks after he was born. Eugénie de Sutre, again according to a Sorrel family historian John Gordon Freymann in "The Sorrel Family in Saint-Domingue" was quite possibly a member of the *gens de couleur libres*, and if true, this would further explain Antoine's championing of their cause. The free people of color in St. Domingue enjoyed many more opportunities in Haiti than did their counterparts in America. There, mulattoes, as they called anyone of mixed parentage, were free to own land and as many slaves as they could afford and were often wealthier than white landowners, so it would not have been unusual for someone of Antoine's station and class to marry a free woman of color. What is known about Eugénie is that she was definitely at the plantation in Miragoâne in the South Province in May of 1793, and she died there on June 23 of the same year and was buried on the plantation.

By the year of François' birth, a tremendous black market for trading with others—the American colonies, the Netherlands, Spain, and Great Britain—had developed in St. Domingue. France's monopoly on the sugar trade created constant international tension in the area and there evolved a perfect environment for corruption and intrigue. Thousands of runaway slaves banded together in the mountains of the region. They wanted equal rights and were determined to get them. After the slave revolt in 1791, the French sent commissioners with troops to try to regain control by courting free blacks and *gens de coleur*. St. Dominique was a cauldron of internal chaos and violence. France and Great Britain declared war, and Great Britain invaded St. Domingue. The execution of Louis XVI increased the tensions in the colony. Slaves slaughtered whites by the thousands, and in an effort to appease them, the French abolished slavery. By 1792, a civil war raged in which French royalist forces likely fought with mulatto and black troops against white republicans, a confusing scenario on all sides.

In June of 1793, just a month after François birth, whites and mulattos faced off as a mulatto army attempted to take the city of Cap François. Whites united and tried to hold their ground, but the mulatto leader promised freedom to all slaves in North Province who joined their cause, and the city was destroyed, sending most whites fleeing. Thus ended white power in St. Domingue. However, "*Antoine Sorrel was a well-known ally of the mulattoes, and his engineering skills and intimate knowledge of the region made him much too valuable to kill just because of the color of his skin."* (Freymann, p. 17)

After François' birth, his father Antione was still a French officer managing a sugar plantation in the South Province. The city of Le Cap was captured the same day Eugénie died. By 1794, the fighting in the South Province had escalated, and the plantations that had survived thus far were destroyed and their inhabitants killed. The Sorrel plantation was probably burned sometime between 1794 and 1795, (the adult Francis told his daughter Aminta that he was four or five years old when the plantation was burned and he was taken to Port-au-Prince) and the British seized the Port-au-Prince townhouse in 1795 while Antoine, according to a complaint filed by his son-in law, was in jail in Léogane, just west of Port-au-Prince. Antoine managed to survive jail and execution and was most likely in Nippes in June of 1796 where, at the habitation of Sorrel's friend, M. Bezin, his son François was baptized on June 28. The brother of Antoine's first wife Perrinette was noted as François' godfather. Antoine had been separated from his infant son shortly after his birth until this baptism three years later. It was shortly after his baptism that the child was most likely placed with relatives in British-held Port-au-Prince, though the identities of these relatives are unknown. Francis Sorrel later told his daughter Aminta that he lived with these relatives, but who could they have been? His older half-sister Bonne had married and moved to France. Though Bonne's husband was probably still in Port-au-Prince, he would surely have sent Bonne to France at the outbreak of violence in St. Domingue. François' half-brother Théodat was eighteen in 1796, so the most likely guardian among known relatives would have been François' godfather Louis François Olliveir du Petit Bois, Antoine's previous brother-in-law who had no children of his own.

Peace returned to the island in the spring of 1798, and regardless of where Antoine had been and what he had been doing for the last couple of years, he became Chief Engineer of the Department of the West, a position that is recorded in the colonial archives in Paris. Peace did not last long, however, and another civil war broke out in June of 1799. Prosperity returned to the island from 1800 to 1801, but there is no evidence that François was living with his father Antoine. The years of peace should have given Antoine a chance to reconnect with his son, but François, who would have been eight years old by then and capable of remembering life with his father, did not recall his father's presence in his life, so Antoine most likely remained absent.

Peace again was short-lived; it ended in 1802 when a 20,000-man French army sent by Napoleon landed on St. Domingue. Antoine was promoted to Colonel of Infantry and Director of the Topographical Bureau. The opposing sides slaughtered indiscriminately, but the French were no match for the virulent yellow fever that was discriminating. In November, 1803, eight thousand survivors evacuated the island. Whether Antoine was among those troops or fled separately is unknown. He shows up in Cuba in 1805. Once again, he had survived, but he had left behind his possessions, the affluent life he had built for himself on the island, and most inexplicably, his ten-year-old son François whom he had probably not seen since François was three. He left François in the newly formed nation of Haiti, but little remained of the once richest colony on earth. François was left to fend for himself in a country ravaged by war and purged almost entirely of the white race.

From Havana, sixty-eight-year-old Antoine contacted his wealthy second cousin, Jacques Joseph Sorrel, then living in Louisiana on the 5000-acre plantation he owned along Bayou Teche. Jacques Joseph and Antoine had grown up together in Grenoble, but Jacques Joseph had gone to Louisiana in 1762, partnered with a man named Gregoire Pellerin, and made a fortune. When Antoine wrote Jacques Joseph asking for asylum, Jacques Joseph sent the son of his deceased partner to Havana to rescue him. Frederic Pellerin took Antoine to New Orleans, a town that had almost doubled in number from the influx of refugees from the West Indies, and from there they traveled up the Bayou to the Sorrel plantation. There he was welcomed warmly by his cousin, given his own body servant, and treated like a member of the family that Jacques Joseph apparently considered him to be. Antoine lived another 25 years on the plantation. His cousin died leaving him an annual income with Frederic Pellerin taking over the role of protector. Pellerin's daughters married Jacques Joseph's nephews Solange and Martial who come to the plantation from France, and they, too, seemed devoted to the aging Antoine. It was Martial who informed Francis that his father Antoine Sorrel had died on May 9, 1830 at the age of 93.

> *"Antoine had had a good life. Granted, he had suffered tragedy during those awful years of war and insurrection, but look at his first 53 years and his last 25! Scion of a prominent family, well-educated, he had been able to practice his profession while enjoying the life of a landed aristocrat for 20 years, thanks to his wife's wealth. He was 53 when that world fell apart. He regained his former way of life when he was 68 and enjoyed it to the age of 93, thanks to the generosity of loving relatives."*
> (Freymann, p. 32)

Antoine's advantages in life came, in great part, from the beneficence of family. The Sorrels in Louisiana provided for his safe passage and his every need. Antoine, on the other hand, seemed to completely forget the young son he had left behind to fend for himself. In March of 1804, the black dictator of independent Haiti set out to eliminate the few whites who had managed to stay alive on the island. Mathurin François Sorrel, an eleven-year-old boy without mother or father was one of those few remaining white people trying to stay alive. How could Antoine Sorrel have left his own son in such a dangerous environment?

The only charitable reasons for Antoine to leave his son were that he thought him dead or he didn't know how to locate him. Both excuses are weak. Antoine would have had to know with whom he left him, and even if he had had to flee for his own life without having time to find his son, this does not explain why he didn't try to locate his child after he was provided safety in America. Jacques Joseph had quickly and compassionately sent help to Antoine when he needed it, so it is hard to believe he would not have sent someone to Haiti to find Antoine's son, even if he had waited until 1806 when the turmoil in Haiti abated and commerce re-opened. There were American merchants doing business with Haiti after 1806, so it would not have been too difficult for Antoine to make inquiries about his son. It would appear that Antoine had no real desire to locate his son and bring him to safety. Why wouldn't Antoine want to save his own son and have him brought to him in America? John Gordon Freymann thinks the only explanation is that his great, great grand-father Francis Sorrel must have been sorely flawed in his own father's eyes.

2

Francis Sorrel
Patriarch of the Sorrels of Savannah

Antoine left François in 1796 to grow up among Eugénie's white relatives in British-held Port-au-Prince. Since those same white relatives appear later in France, they must have fled Saint Domingue no later than March of 1804, when François was only eleven years old. How the light-skinned François managed to escape the fate of most other whites in the region will never be known. If François' relatives were free people of color, those remaining on the island might have taken the boy in—they would have had a better chance of survival because, with so few whites left, mulattos emerged as the new aristocracy of Haiti. (Freymann, p. 47). However, even the lives of that class were threatened, especially if they appeared white, as in all likelihood they did because François himself had no trouble "passing" for white.

Francis Sorrel, Patriarch of the Sorrels of Savannah

Regardless of François' class in Haiti, the young boy would have had to witness much violence and death before leaving for the United States. In a letter to R. H. Douglass dated 1818 he writes, *"Born in a country savaged by many cruel and bloody revolutions, I was separated from my parents at an early age; left alone amidst corruption..."* and according to accounts written by his children, he became greatly distressed when the subject of his early life was broached by them or anyone else. Consequently, he took the details of what really happened to him to his grave. Somehow, young François managed to survive until he was fourteen years old, at which time, according to his daughter Aminta in "A Short Sketch of the Life of Francis Sorrel of Savannah, Georgia," François, *"having only the rudiments of an education...and being absolutely without means,"* decided he would have to find a way to take care of himself. Though he spoke only French, he gained employment in a counting house owned by brothers Richard H. and George Douglass, two Maryland coffee and sugar traders who had an office in Haiti. François became the chief clerk in their Port-au-Prince office. By 1811, François had become the administrative secretary and temporary public registrar in Port-au-Prince at just eighteen years old.

It was also in 1811 that Richard Henry Douglass moved his primary offices to Baltimore, Maryland, and became the only principal in his own firm. At Richard's invitation nineteen-year-old François sailed to America in 1812 to work in that office. Upon arriving, Richard Douglass sent him to live with a clergyman in order to learn English. In the letter from Baltimore to Richard dated February of 1818, François signs his name as "Francis" and gladly accepts the position as the head of a new mercantile house in Savannah proclaiming,

> *"Wherever you will please send me to: I shall willingly go, if it is to promote your interest, but let Port au Prince be the last place; I have a complete aversion for Haiti; the state of that country is too precarious."*

By the year 1818, François had Americanized his name to Francis Sorrel, and he and Richard Douglass were partners in the firm *Douglass and Sorrel* in Savannah, Georgia. Advertisements in the local newspapers listed merchandise such as whiskey, butter, corn, and flour for sale at different wharfs by the firm of *Douglass and Sorrel* in 1818, and they were still doing business with coffee merchants in Port-au- Prince in 1821 as evidenced by the advertisement of Haitian coffee for sale and accommodations for passengers on the schooner Major Croghan that would be returning to Port-au- Prince. Francis' dedication to Douglass and the company is made evident in a letter from a Mr. Richardson dated 1820 during the first horrific yellow fever epidemic to hit Savannah. The city had also been devastated by fire earlier that year, and people fled the city in droves. Francis refused to leave the business unattended. Richardson writes Richard Douglass:

> *"I wrote a very particular letter to Sorrell (sic) beg-*
> *ging him not to remain & stating that neither you*
> *nor his correspondents could expect under such cir-*
> *cumstances & that certainly it was not rendered*
> *incumbent on him by his official situation in the*
> *Bank. He replied that with his clerk sick he could*
> *not think of leaving the property committed to his*
> *charge and relied on Providence & his precautions*
> *against sickness. His motive was highly to be ap-*
> *plauded, but…the fever having become worse when*
> *I last wrote him.….I could not help reiterating what*
> *I had before said…"*

What Mr. Richardson couldn't have known was that Francis realized he was in little danger of the disease as he had long before developed an immunity to it while living in Haiti. However, this documentation is early evidence of a business savvy along with dedication and drive that would eventually make Francis a very wealthy, respected businessman in Savannah.

Francis prospered as a shipper and tradesman and was appointed Portuguese Vice Consul for Georgia possibly as early as 1816—his name shows up in a court case involving a slave ship, *The Antelope*, that had been pirated, then confiscated on behalf of the United States off the coast of Florida for suspicion of slave trafficking. Francis

Sorrel is listed as the Vice Counsel of Portugal who sues for the return of the slaves who had been pirated from the Portuguese. (Case of the Antelope otherwise the Ramirez and Cargo, May 11, 1821; Vol. 103, Minute Book 1816-1823, Div. Savannah, GA; Off. Circuit Courts; Records Group 21, United States District Court; National Archives and Records Administration—Southeast Region, Atlanta).

How Francis came to be the Vice Counsel to Portugal is, like many other aspects of his life, unknown. It is evidence, however, that the young clerk quickly did well for himself in his adopted country. Francis was sworn in as a United States Citizen on July 8, 1824, by an order entered by Judge James M. Wayne in the Superior Court of Chatham County, Georgia, a man whose friendship and support Francis would enjoy for many years to come. By 1825 Francis had dissolved his partnership with Douglass and was in business on his own. Francis also partnered with George W. Anderson, but that company was dissolved in 1831. The Francis Sorrel Company, supplied oats, coffee, sugar, whiskey, wine, beef, and other staples. He was also the agent for Savannah & Charleston Packet Co. He built a four-story office complex, Sorrel Block, on the corner of Bay and Bull Streets across from the Customs House, the rent from which he and his children benefited until 1908 when it was sold. The sturdy building is still in good condition today.

As to Francis' relationship with his father, letters to

and by Richard Douglass reveal that Francis knew of his father's location in Bayou Teche before he left Haiti and hoped to meet him there. For whatever reason, they would never meet again in life, though Francis acknowledges writing his father before leaving Haiti in response to Richard Douglass' correspondence. The young man must have received no encouragement from his father in Louisiana. In later years they corresponded some, but Antoine never overtly recognized his son François, and he left everything he owned when he died to the husband of his daughter by his first marriage who had been in an asylum for the mentally ill for most of her adult life. His son by his first marriage had died in early adulthood.

Though Francis was not yet wealthy while his father lived, he certainly had the means to visit family and friends, yet he never chose to visit his father in Bayou Teche. Francis Sorrel named each of his eleven children after relatives and friends he respected and loved. The name Antoine is revealingly absent in his offspring.

Antoine's family and friends in Louisiana noted his neglect of his family in Savannah and found it odd. Though Antoine loved to talk about his first wife and his daughter Bonne, he was strangely silent about his second wife and the child she bore him. In a letter to one of Francis' son, the great-grandson of Antoine's friend and benefactor Pellerin comments,

" ...the Louisiana Sorrels thought Mr. Sorrel's neglect of his second family and the stubborn silence he affected in reference to it was quite strange. He hardly spoke of it, avoided conversation on the subject, at least with his relatives, dodged every question. Never would he mention or even indicate in any way the background, the name of his second wife..."

If François' mother truly were a free person of color, this would explain his father's reluctance to acknowledge his first wife or his son by her when he first came to America. Mixed race could have been the perceived flaw that would have made his own father desert him. Though marriage to a person with mixed blood had been acceptable in Haiti, it certainly would not have been in the United States where even the hint of black blood would have classified his wife and son as members of the black race. He undoubtedly would have been ostracized by the white gentry he considered his contemporaries. François himself certainly did not disclose his heritage when he came to America, either. It would have been societal suicide for him to do so, and he certainly would not have been welcomed into the slaveholding Douglass and Moxley families of Virginia into which he married.

Whatever the reasons, it is obvious that father and son rejected a relationship with each other. It would appear that the son's indifference to his father stemmed from his father's desertion and denial of his existence. In 1830, possibility of a reconciliation between the two men came to an end when Francis received word from his cousin Martial Sorrel that his father had died. In a letter, Martial writes, *"My brother and myself, who loved him as a father and reverenced him as a being on earth the living image of the goodness of heaven, have deeply felt his loss."*

The last news Francis had of his father was that the man who gave him life had been more of a father to his cousins than he had been to him, a sad closure to what had been a sad chapter of his life.

In sailing to America, it appeared that Francis had left behind him all hardships and privation associated with his early life. Though he would no longer have to worry about bodily sustenance, Francis would continue to suffer heartache in love. Not only would he never reunite with his father, his mother's early death seemed to set the stage for his luck with women.

Upon first arriving in America, happenstance and the need to find a place to stay in which the proprietors spoke French led him to a boarding house run by a Mme. Anne Laval. This fortuitous meeting, later related by Francis' daughter's Aminta, is one of the few existing clues to the identity of Eugénie, Francis' mother. Aminta claims that Mme. Laval was actually Francis' aunt, the sister of Eugénie. Mme. Laval's husband had supposedly been killed in the French Revolution, and she and her daughter Rodolphine maintained a boarding house in Baltimore to make ends meet. Though younger than his first cousin, Francis reportedly fell in love with her and used part of his hard-earned wages to better her life. Francis lost out to a young naval officer named Alexander Claxton whom Rodolphine married, but Francis and his cousin remained lifelong friends, and Francis valued both her friendship and the friendship of her husband so much that he would later name a daughter after Rodolphine and a son after Alexander Claxton.

Francis would marry twice and father eleven children; eight would live to adulthood. Though Francis would suffer sadness in both his marriages, his position in the community of Savannah and the state of Georgia was one of trust, prosperity, and affluence. He was the chairman of the board of trustees of The Independent Presbyterian Church for thirty years, and upon his death, they erected a plaque in his honor. He was involved in charitable works, business organizations, and government in Savannah. Records show that Francis was a stockholder and member of the board of directors for The Planter's Bank for forty years, the president of which, George W. Anderson, was a personal friend and administrator of his affairs; he was an agent and treasurer of the Savannah & Charleston Steam Packet; and he was a stockholder for Central Railroad and Banking Company of Savannah Georgia. He was listed as an appointed commissioner on more than one act established by the state legislature in Milledgeville, one in 1835 incorporating the Savannah Poor House and Hospital of which he was one of its earliest patrons, and another in 1833 establishing a waterline for the wharfs along the Savannah River and establishing Canal Street. He acted as a Justice of the Inferior Court of Chatham County for several years. He was on a "steering committee" appointed by The Ladies Gunboat Association and was one of those responsible for getting the confederate gunboat *Georgia* constructed. (Mark Swanson, Robert Holcombe, CSS Georgia: Archival Study, U.S. Army Corps of Engineers, Jan. 31, 2007) Though he apparently retired from business in the late 1850's (Dun and Bradstreet Collection, Francis Sorrel: 54), he was still a wealthy man by 1860 when the

census reveals real estate holdings of $55,000 and personal estate holdings of $60,000.

A letter written to his son Frank in 1870 reveals him to be of sound mind and still living at the time with daughters Lucy and Annie in the house he built next door to the Sorrel House in the mid 1850's. Less than two months later on May 5, 1870, the day after his 77th birthday, he died at

An Elderly Francis Sorrel

home *"peacefully passing away encircled by children and friends" three days after suffering a stroke"* (handwritten family record). In honor of his place in the community, *"many of the stores of his tenants on the Bay were closed, and the city court adjourned in order to allow the members of the Bar opportunity to participate in the sad ceremonies."* ("A Short Sketch…" Aminta Sorrel) The funeral was conducted by his good friend Pastor I.S.K. Axson. Francis was buried in the vault with his wife Matilda at Laurel Grove Cemetery, just feet from the grave of his first wife Lucy.

It appears the sisters would share him in death as they had life.

The Sorrel Block built by Francis Sorrel on the corner of Bay and Bull Streets, as it appears today

3

The Douglass Sisters

Lucinda Ireland Moxley Sorrel

Francis' relationship with the Douglass brothers brought him into contact with Lucinda Ireland Moxley who was attending school in Baltimore. She was the second child of the late Gilbert Ireland Moxley and Aminta E. Douglass, the sister of Richard Henry and George Douglass, Francis' long-time business associates. Lucinda and her sisters were well-connected on their father's side as well as on their mother's. Their grandfather, Alvin Moxley, was *"one of the signers of what is known as the Richard Lee Bill of Rights, 1765, the first recorded protest in America against taxation without representation, and which, twelve years later, led directly to the Revolutionary War."* (Moxley Sorrel, *Recollections of a Confederate Staff Officer*, p. 20) Lucinda was named after her father's youngest sister Lucy. Gilbert died at the age of thirty-three, probably from tuberculosis, and left 1/7 of his land and 1/3 of his personal property to his wife Aminta, and the remainder of his estate was to be divided equally among his children alive at that time. Besides Lucinda and Matilda, there was an

older sister Anne Dent Douglass Moxley, a younger sister Sophia Mary Parnham Moxley, and a younger brother Benjamin Gustavus Douglass Moxley who was just two-years-old at the time of his father's death. Gilbert's untimely death left Aminta with five children to provide and care for, all of them younger than ten years old. Aminta was not destitute, however. Records show that she inherited 1,920 acres in Illinois to be split with her sister, and an 1840 census showed Mrs. Moxley still living on the family estate in Virginia, The Grove, and owning thirteen slaves. So the twenty-nine-year-old Francis, in all likelihood, acquired property in Virginia when he married the seventeen-year-old Lucinda. They married on September 6, 1822, in what was then Washington City to avoid the appointing of a guardian for the underage Lucy as required in her home state of Virginia. They set up housekeeping in

Savannah and had three children, a girl and two boys. Lucinda served as Secretary of the Female Missionary Society of Savannah in 1824, the same year Francis became an American citizen.

On November of 1827, tragedy took a woman whom Francis loved. Just three months after the birth of their third child, Lucinda con-tracted yellow fever, pur-

**Aminta Elizabeth
Douglass Moxley
Mother of Lucinda & Matilda**

portedly while nursing neighbors in yet another Savannah epidemic. She died and was buried in the Laurel Grove Cemetery beside what would become the Francis Sorrel vault. Upon her tombstone is inscribed an epitaph penned by the Honorable Henry Wilde, an intimate friend:

> *Possessed of a soul Pure, Generous and Noble*
> *A heart embued with Piety,*
> *She resigned to the summons of the Redeemer,*
> *and Religion sheds its Luster o'er her Grave.*
> *Affection bleeds, and Charity laments,*
> *While recording her lost name on earth.*

The death of the young Lucinda inspired yet another poetic tribute. A Savannah newspaper ran the following:

The Complaint

Ah me! How blithesome were the hours
When love and youth old time beguiled:
Now the dark cloud of sorrow lowers
Where once all nature round me smil'd.
'Tis thus our gravest moments glide
Fast as the tide or vagrant wind.
The highest bliss to pain allied—
Leaves but mem'ry's dream behind.

Matilda Ann Douglass Moxley Sorrel

Lucinda's death left Francis Sorrel a thirty-four-year-old widower with three young children in Savannah, no relatives of his own, and far from Lucinda's family in Virginia. Not quite two years after Lucy's death, Francis remedied his problem by marrying Lucy's younger sister Matilda who was twenty-three years old to Francis' thirty-six. This marriage should have provided Francis with another 1/7 of the original Gilbert Moxley estate in Virginia; therefore, Ireland, the family place they owned and at which they summered in Virginia, was most likely the land his two wives inherited upon the death of their father Gilbert Moxley. Together, Francis and Matilda had eight children, only five of whom survived.

By all indications, Francis and Matilda shared several good years, and there is no evidence that theirs was not a union of mutual love and respect. However, there is evidence that Matilda suffered from prolonged bouts of depression and mental instability, and on March 27, 1860, she fell from a balcony to her death. One family account claims that Matilda fainted causing the fall, but that is unlikely. The most likely scenario is found in the compilation of letters written during that time entitled *Children of Pride*. Charles Colcock, Jr. writes in a letter to his mother Mary that Matilda threw herself *"in a moment of lunacy"* (Charles Colcock, p. 570) from an upstairs porch of their home, *"falling upon the pavement of the yard, and by the concussion terminating her life"* (p. 571), thereby continuing Francis' legacy of tragic loss. Mary Jones, Charles' mother writes back to her son *"The death of Mrs. Sorrel was very distressing. I heard some time since that she was subject to great mental depressions."* (p. 572) Little else regarding the cause of her death can be found. Matilda's death inspired no poetic tributes as had her sister's, but all three of her daughters, Lucy, Agnes, and Annie, named daughters Matilda after her death as Aminta, her stepdaughter as well as her niece, had done while she was living. All must have been greatly impacted by her death and the manner in which it happened, yet each chose to honor her by keeping her name alive in her offspring.

Francis, too, clearly mourned her loss and continued to hold his wife in high regard. In a letter to his son Claxton written in October of 1860 from their country home Ireland in Virginia, Francis tells of a visit he is enjoying from their friends the Axsons, and he writes,

"How my dear & beloved wife would have enjoyed the visit of our friends, if her life had been preserved!! ....and how much more comfortable she would have made them than I have been enabled to do!!....But I must not enlarge on this sorrowful subject. The Lord has bereaved us and laid his chastening rod heavily upon me, and I must submit."

Though successful, even powerful, in business as well as popular and influential in Savannah society, personal happiness in romantic love was not destined for Francis. Though Francis lived another ten years, he did not remarry. Perhaps he was unwilling to risk the loss of yet another woman he loved.

4

The Children of Francis and Lucinda Sorrel

Aminta Elizabeth Douglass Sorrel

The first of the Sorrel children was Aminta Elizabeth Douglass, born on July 8, 1823, not quite a year after Lucinda and Francis were married. She was born in Prince William County, Virginia at the home of Lucy's mother. It was common in the South at that time to name children after relatives or friends, and often they chose to replicate the complete name of the person to be honored; thus, all of the Sorrel children received the full names of their namesakes, giving most of them quite lengthy names, as in the case of Aminta who is given Lucy's mother's full maiden name. It is not surprising that Lucy would choose to name her first born after her mother as her father had died at the age of 34 leaving their mother to raise

Aminta Sorrel Mackall

Lucy and her three sisters and one brother. The matriarch of the family was a staunch Presbyterian and one of the original founders of the Independent Presbyterian Church in Greenwich, Virginia, and her religious influence was seen in Francis as well as her daughters. Though Francis was reared a Catholic, he switched his affiliation to the Independent Presbyterian Church in Savannah where he became a deacon and a major contributor for the rest of his life. The seeds of this allegiance were no doubt planted by the senior Aminta and her brothers Richard Henry and George Douglass, also strong Presbyterians Her namesake, the younger Aminta, would later become the source of much information about her father Francis. Being the oldest child, Francis confided in her throughout his life, and she made an effort to record some of the information he related to her. Being four years old when her mother died, Aminta would be the only child who could have possibly remembered her mother Lucinda.

At the age of sixteen, Aminta was attending school in

Baltimore while staying with her mother's sister Sophia Mary Moxley Fisher. While with them, Aminta met William Whann Mackall, a West Point graduate, while vacationing in New Port, Rhode Island in the summer of 1843. She caught her first glimpse of her future husband from her window as the young lieutenant rode by on horseback. A Captain Clark brought him to visit the Gardners where she was, and she writes in her "Sketch of the Life of Your Father," "*I left engaged, but being an entire stranger it was broke off by my father until he could be satisfied...who he was and his character.*"

Francis must have found the young Mackall satisfactory because they were married in the parlor of the Sorrel House on May 7, 1844 when she was 21 years old. At this time Lieutenant Mackall was already a seasoned military man having been wounded while fighting Indians is the West. He fought in the Mexican War as a member of the United States Army until the outbreak of the

**Brigadier General
William Whann Mackall**

Civil War. Though he thought it was wrong for the South to secede from the Union (he thought the war should have been fought on behalf of both sides under the Stars and Stripes), his allegiance lay with his and his wife's own slaveholding relatives. He gave up his position in the U.S. Army, and he and his family crossed the Potomac at Port Tobacco, Maryland. They were members of the last group of Southerners to cross the river before the Union closed it. Once in the South, Mackall fought under the leadership of Jefferson Davis even though there was a *"long-standing estrangement"* between the two. Family lore claims Mackall caught Davis cheating at cards when they were both young men, but there is nothing concrete to substantiate that claim. Mackall was captured by the Union Army and imprisoned at Ft. Warren until he was exchanged in 1863 and returned to service.

Because William Mackall was away from home so much throughout the first twenty years or so of his marriage, Aminta and their children were often at home at the Sorrel House with her family, at William's father's place at Langley in Virginia, or traveling around the country to be with William. She gave birth to eleven children, five of whom lived to adulthood. Her first child, a son, died at birth or in infancy, Her second child, a daughter, arrived prematurely while she, under escort of her brother Douglass, was sailing home to Savannah on the steamer Rivannah from the garrison at which her husband was stationed in Florida following the outbreak of the Mexican

War. She named her Frances Sorrel Mackall (Fannie), and it was with her that she was living at Langley when she died.

Aminta lost two more children between 1849 and 1851, both girls, Sally Maffit and Matilda Sorrel whom she named after her stepmother/aunt Matilda, an indication that she was close to the woman who reared her. She then gave birth to William Whann Mackall II. (She named her first two living children after her father and her husband, clearly the two most important men in her life.) William Whann II would one day publish a book entitled *A Son's Recollections of His Father* which was privately printed. The next child they named Benjamin, and he grew up to be a Civil Engineer. He had a penchant for genealogy and made a concerted effort to leave behind an accurate history of the Mackall family to date. Aminta and William had a son in '57 (Henry Covington) and another in '59 (Francis L), but both died within two days of each other in '59 and were buried in San Francisco, California. (Another family source lists Francis L.'s birth as 1847, and if that documentation is true, he would have been born the year after the daughter Frances and would have been 12 years old at his death in 1859.) Another surviving son, Douglass Sorrel Mackall, was born in 1863 in Macon, Georgia, the same year his father was imprisoned in Ft. Warren, and he lived to adulthood, but a son (Moxley Sorrel) born a year or two later died at the age of one or two.

The whole Mackall family were reunited and living at

the Vineville, Georgia home of her brother Douglass in 1864. Their last, another son, Henry Clinton Mackall, was born in 1866 in the comfort of their home in Langley, Virginia, and he lived to old age.

According to William Whann II, his parents had a wonderful marriage of mutual respect and romantic devotion. Aminta seemed to be a resourceful woman who, often alone, dealt with the heartache of losing several children and held their family together during the Civil War, providing for her children and household of slaves while there was little to be had in the way of resources. She was a stockholder, along with her father and mother, of Planter's Bank in Savannah, and she was one of the founding members of the The Ladies Gunboat Association that raised money for the construction of the gunboat *Georgia* that her father helped finance at the beginning of the Civil War. She remained a devoted daughter to her father until his death and a loyal wife until William's death in 1891 at Langley. She died in 1904 at Langley, Fairfax County, Virginia, and was buried beside her husband in the Levinsville Presbyterian Cemetery in McLean, Virginia in Fairfax County.

Richard Henry Douglass Sorrel

Douglass as a child

On February 7, 1825, Lucinda and Francis' second child, a son, was born, and they named him Richard Henry Douglass after Francis' mentor and Lucinda's maternal uncle. This honor is not surprising as Francis undoubtedly felt he owed much of his success, and possibly even his life, to the elder Mr. Douglass. Had it not been for him, Francis might never have made the voyage to the United States, and it would have been unlikely that he would have met Lucinda.

Douglass, as he was called by his family, seemed to have inherited some of his Grandfather Antoine's wanderlust and less of his namesake Richard Henry Douglass' business acumen. Douglass must have been a bright boy because he was admitted into the sophomore class at Princeton where he stayed but a short time due to misconduct. He was suspended just a month after his arrival for *"intoxication,"* and *"directed to return home"* just two months after that at the old age of seventeen. In 1850 he was a member of his father's household in Savannah and a bank officer at Planter's Bank, a job he most likely attained through his father's affiliation and friendship with the president George W. Anderson.

Douglas met the young widow Martha Elizabeth Gordon Bell at a resort near Atlanta. She was the daughter of immensely wealthy planter and landowner General John W. Gordon who had resettled his family in Texas after exhausting his plantations in Georgia. The couple married in 1854 in Atlanta just months after meeting, and through her, he acquired immediate and vast wealth. In the 1850's, Douglass moved his wife and first child to Texas to a large plantation on Caney Creek in Wharton County that Martha received as a gift from her father. The Sorrel plantation boasted 1,000 acres of land that produced 7,000 bushels of corn and 300 bales of cotton through the efforts of 123 slaves in 1860. In addition to the plantation, Douglass bought land in Macon and built a fine home in an affluent section called Vineville

Martha Gordon Sorrel

where the large family lived much of the time while Douglass ran the plantation in Texas.

Douglass was drawn away from the plantation for part of the Civil War in which he was a captain in the Ladies' Rangers, thus named because the company was equipped through contributions from patriotic ladies of Houston and Galveston. Douglass probably saw little actual fighting as his role and that of his fellow servicemen seemed to be of a provisionary nature. The task of providing food and supplies for the Confederate army would not have been an easy one, especially by the end of the war. He returned to his plantation when the war ended but was forced into bankruptcy, one would presume, by the devastation of war to the plantation and the pecuniary loss of 123 slaves liberated by Lincoln's Emancipation Proclamation and enforced by the Union Army. Most of his plantation was sold at auction, yet it was actually bought by his wife Martha for the deflated price of a little over twenty-four dollars. Martha apparently had retained money of her own, and wisely so, as Douglass had already defaulted on the property they owned in Macon and been bailed out by his father Francis who had bought the place at auction and returned it to his son. However, records show that Francis bought the property again just months after the first bail out, but this time he put it in his son Moxley's name to hold in trust for Douglass' wife and children. The instructions were explicit—the land was to and for the *"benefit and behoof of Martha E. Sorrel... for and during the term of her natural life free from debts, contracts or control of the said R. H. Douglass Sorrel or of any husband with whom she may hereafter intermarry....then to for and amongst the children of the said Martha E. and R. H. Douglass..."*

Apparently, the restrictions accomplished what Francis had intended because Martha retained the Vineville property until after the children were grown, selling it in 1887.

In 1868, Francis financially distanced himself from his son Douglass in his last will and testament, a few months before Douglass' bankruptcy filing. Francis writes in his own hand,

"In consequence of the pecuniary embarrassments of my son R. H. Douglass Sorrel, ...I hereby direct, that the shares of my Estate which would fall to him, should he survive me, shall be held In Trust....for the sole use and benefit of the children of my son Douglass,....and not subject to the debts, contracts, or control of my said son Douglass."

The term "pecuniary embarrassments" was an indictment on his son's money handling skills, and the will made it impossible for Douglass' hovering debtors to claim part of Francis' estate. These precautions along with the earlier appointing of Moxley as guardian over the Vineville place were meant to insure some kind of security for Douglass' wife and children. It is obvious that Francis had lost faith in his son's ability to support himself and take care of his family, a situation probably made even more frustrating for Francis by the fact that his son Douglass had squandered and misman-

Douglass Sorrel

aged money simply handed to him by his father-in-law, while he, Francis, was a self-made man.

Douglass had six children to whom he passed on family names including that of his father. His second son he named Francis Des Rivieres, calling attention to his father's French ancestry. His first daughter he named Aminta Douglass Sorrel after his maternal grandmother (and possibly his sister), but she died at the age of five in Macon, Georgia, the cause listed as diarrhea. His youngest daughter he named Moxley after his mother's family and possibly his younger brother who had by that time become quite well known for his role in the Civil War, and his fourth son he named Marcial Sorrel after his grandfather

Antoine's cousin, the uncle of whom, Jacques Joseph, had given Antoine a home on his Louisiana plantation when he was forced to leave St. Domingue. This last name is of interest because it makes one think that Douglass reconnected with his grandfather's people in a way that Francis had been unwilling to do.

Douglass barely survived his father. Family lore claims that Douglass ate tainted fish while buying supplies in Galveston but made it back to his plantation where he died in 1871, the exact date uncertain, at the age of 46. He was buried on the Sorrel plantation . His early death delivered him from the heartache that his wife Martha would have to face alone. Their two old-

An older Douglas Sorrel

est sons, John Gordon (Frenchie) Sorrel and Francis Des Rivieres Sorrel died in 1876 at just 21 and 19 years old. The first was killed in an ambush and the second died of jaundice, probably hepatitis. Three of their children lived to adulthood: a son Marcial, a daughter Moxley, and his namesake, Richard H. D. Sorrel II who would later become a Wharton County State legislator. The Sorrel Plantation flourished under Richard H. D. Sorrel, II's management.

Even though Douglass was not the businessman most of his ancestors had been, he left a Sorrel legacy in Texas, and he and his offspring are an important part of that state's history.

Louis Francis Mathurin Sorrel

Dr. Frank Sorrel

The third and last child of Francis and Lucinda was Louis Francis Mathurin, born July 28, 1827. He was only three months old when Lucinda died. Named after his father, he became known as Frank. According to a memorial written by Aminta's husband W. W. Mackall, Frank Sorrel was quite a picturesque character, and he had definitely inherited his Grandfather Antoine's love of adventure. Frank followed his older brother to Princeton where he experienced much greater educational success. He graduated at the age of nineteen and went on to get a medical degree from the University of Pennsylvania. After graduation, the adventurous Frank decided to improve himself by "travel and observation." He took advantage of his family connections, especially those in France, and he met members of the aristocracy and made acquaintances of such interesting character that the profession of town doctor soon lost its appeal. He practiced medicine out of the basement of the Sorrel House, using a gateway in the brick wall on Bull Street as an entrance for patients. His adventuresome nature led him to be the second in a duel for his soon-to-be brother-in-law Stewart Elliot, Frank's younger sister Lucy's husband.

After just a few years, Francis, Jr. gave up his practice in Savannah and accepted a commission as surgeon in the United States Army, serving with distinction in the battles with indigenous Indians disturbing the peace of whites who had chosen to claim Indian land as their own in Florida. Hearing tales of gold and adventure in the West, Frank applied for duty in California. In the early 1850's, Frank became part of California history by teaming up with three other men to save Fort Jones, an outpost in Siskiyou County set up to protect miners from Indian attack. The post was about to go under when Lt. George Crook, a versatile hunter; 2nd Lt. John B. Hood, an experienced farmer who would later become well-known for his leadership in the Civil War; 1st Lt. John Bonnycastle; and Assistant Surgeon Francis Sorrel, a good businessman, came up with a scheme to provide not only food for the camp but a money-making service for themselves. Through raising crops and killing game, they sustained themselves and the outpost. Sorrel's role was selling the game in the town of Yreka, sixteen miles from Fort Jones. This revenue helped them pay their other bills and buy ammunition and other supplies cheaper in the San Francisco Market than through their quartermaster. (Hart,

Colonel Herbert M. (retired) Executive Director, Council on America's Military Past, The California State Military Museum) Apparently, the junior Francis had inherited his father's good business sense.

By 1860 Frank was back in San Francisco, California, as a civilian where he located himself in one of the largest mining camps and set up a lucrative medical practice, many of his fees being paid in gold dust. Because of his skill as a surgeon and his winsome personality, Frank was popular with the locals, and in 1860-61, he was elected a member of the Legislature of California. He, like most of his family members, was a strong proponent for Southern secession and as a member of the Legislature, he voted for secession, but as history reveals, the ordinance was defeated. Realizing that the Southern Cause on the West Coast was lost, he resigned the legislature and headed south to fight the North with his own people. He traveled across the West, and after weeks of danger and mishap, he reached Richmond where he was commissioned a surgeon in the Southern Army. (W. W. Mackall, "The Late Doctor Francis Sorrel," The Georgia Historical Quarterly, p. 33-34) He was rapidly promoted. His brother Moxley in *Recollections of a Confederate Staff Officer* writes of his brother's advancement and influence in the Confederacy:

> *"Dr. Moore, the confederate Surgeon-General had him appointed to full rank and assigned for service as his close confidential assistant (the pair were*

forever rolling cigarettes). There his influence and power were considerable and the Doctor was always helpful to his friends....He kept a good lookout for his two junior brothers in the field and we had many evidences of his thoughtfulness." (p. 58)

Dr. Sorrel, along with his brother-in-law William Whann Mackall, was instrumental in getting his young brother Claxton a commission, and his influential contacts, like that of his old friend John B. Hood, helped both of his brothers in their advancement.

"With a wide acquaintance in Richmond, he knew the principal members of Congress and was liked by all the Cabinet. His previous service in the United States Army put him in good touch with many high officers, and his position in all respects was enviable. Occasionally, I managed to make a short visit to Richmond, and then my brother gave introductions to pleasant men and charming women." (p. 59)

Dr. Frank Sorrel moved in powerful circles, his connections going all the way to the top of the Confederate hierarchy, and he included Moxley, who was often stationed close by, in gatherings in Richmond.

"On one of my visits to the city I was persuaded by my brother, Dr. Sorrel, to stay the night and

*attend a reception at the President's. It was interest-
ing and striking. The highest and most brilliant of
the Southland were there, bright, witty, confident,
carrying everything with a high hand....After pre-
sentation to Mr. And Mrs. Davis, I had a good
look at that remarkable man..."* (p. 68-69)

Francis Sorrel senior had taught his sons to *"make friends
always and by all means,"* and this was a lesson well-learned
by them. By the end of the war, Frank was in line for a
promotion to the position of Surgeon General.

Dr. Sorrel, his lust for adventure apparently somewhat
sated by the end of the war, married Mrs. Rives, originally
Miss Letitia Gamble Watts (Lettie) on March 11, 1865,
at her estate in Roanoke, Virginia, and thereafter he was
known as *"Uncle Frank of Roanoke"* to his siblings' children. His brother Moxley convalesced at Roanoke from a
wound he received in battle, and, while there, he acted as
Frank's best man. Frank and Lettie lived on her estate until
her death. His married life was reputed to be extremely
happy, but their union resulted in no children, and her
death in 1900 was a blow from which he reportedly never
recovered. He disposed of her Virginia estate and moved
to Washington City to be close to family and the many
friends he had made throughout his long, eventful life. He
was known to be a wonderful storyteller and a delightful
companion. He died on June 30, 1916, just days shy of his
90th birthday in Washington, District of Columbia.

5

The Children of Francis and Matilda Sorrel

Lucinda Ireland Moxley Sorrel

Matilda gave birth to a daughter a little over two years after she married Francis, and they named her in honor of Francis' first wife and Matilda's dead sister. A handwritten Sorrel family record documents Lucinda's birth at about 1:30 p.m. on January 28, 1831, in Savannah. More than one source lists her year of birth as 1829, but this is highly unlikely because Francis and Matilda were not married until March of 1829. Regardless, from all accounts, she was a spunky child who grew into a beautiful, talented young lady who played with the hearts of many of Savannah's young men. In a letter to her sister Aminta away at school, her father jests that eight-year-old Lucy *"has received from the young beaux"* so many invitations that she in most likelihood will be voted *"Queen of May."* Francis had no way of knowing at that time how true his reflections would prove to be.

Lucinda Ireland Moxley Sorrel became the youngest in the line of four women named Lucinda. The first known to be given the name was Lucinda Moxley, the sister of Gilbert Ireland Moxley, father of Francis Sorrel's wives' Lucinda and Matilda. The second was Lucinda Ireland Moxley Douglass, the above-mentioned first wife of Francis Sorrel. Therefore, Lucinda Ireland Moxley Sorrel was named after both her great-aunt and her aunt. This Lucy's aunt Anne Douglass Hunton, the second Lucinda's sister, added to the confusion by naming her daughter Lucinda Ireland Hunton after their mutual aunt and her own sister. If that scenario were not confusing enough, Charles Green, the neighbor and good friend to the Sorrels, married as his second wife Lucy Ireland Hunton, so, not only were Francis and Charles Green life-long friends, they were related by marriage. Both Green's wife Lucy and Francis' daughter Lucy shared the same grandmother, Mrs. Aminta Moxley, who lived in Virginia. It is this Charles Green, Francis's dear friend and his nephew by marriage, who provides us with our best insight to the youngest Lucinda Sorrel. In a letter to Mrs. Aminta Moxley, his grandmother-in-law, he writes of Francis and Matilda's daughter Lucy:

"...Lucy Sorrel, after flirting and amusing herself at the expense of others, has at last been caught herself. A certain Mr. Elliot here, of more notoriety than fame, and of more talent than grace, who has been closely attentive to her all winter, has formally avowed himself, & poor Lucy dreadfully infatuated, accepted him on Saturday night but to dismiss him under the agitated remonstrances of father, mother and brothers on Sunday. I did not believe she would have submitted but she did—and wrote the gentleman a letter which if she abides by, will raise her higher in my estimation than she has ever stood before. She looks as tho' she has gone thro' a crucible of trouble, as no doubt she has, for she loved the man intensely."

This excerpt speaks to many aspects of Lucy's nature. It notes that she has long trifled with the affections of men interested in her, that she has a strong will, but that she also desires the approval of her parents and brothers. As of the date of the letter, Lucy was 25 years old and legally capable of marrying anyone she chose. However, Charles Green's surprise that she had *"submitted"* proved to be warranted as well, since Lucy did indeed marry Daniel Stewart Elliot on June 1, 1858, two years after she had acquiesced to her family's wishes and rejected him. Too, Lucy had not chosen to marry him at last because of an improvement in his reputation. Though Stewart

Elliot was the son of the wealthy and respected John and Martha Elliot of Savannah, his personal reputation, already somewhat sullied at the time of his first proposal in 1856, was even more blackened by what some considered the murder of former friend Thomas S. Daniell. Daniell was the son of a prominent physician and former mayor of the city, Dr. William C. Daniell. Thomas S. Daniell challenged Elliot to a dual over some minor incident that originated at the Chatham Club, a local drinking establishment where young, wealthy rowdies socialized and played billiards and cards. There are many accounts of the famous duel, but all seem to agree that Elliot tried to resolve the argument peacefully, but that Daniell, known for being involved in other duels, refused to be mollified. Lucy's brother Frank was a close friend of Elliot's and acted as a second in the duel. Their nephew, Aminta's son, William Whann Mackall, Jr. wrote an account of the duel in *A Son's Recollections of His Father.*

> *"It was during his (Frank's) sojourn in Savannah that the famous duel between Mr. Stuart Elliott, and Captain Daniels (resulting in the death of the latter) occurred. My uncle was an intimate friend of Elliott, and served as his second. The meeting took place in the early morning, on the South Carolina side of the Savannah River. Daniel was a nefarious duelist and an expert with fire-arms. The duel was forced on Elliott who with his friends*

made every effort to adjust the affair in a man-
ner honorable to both parties and without resort
to the arbitrament of arms, but Daniels was ob-
durate and insisted on the meeting, and being the
challenged party selected rifles as the weapons to be
used. At the first fire, Elliott shot into the air, and
the ball from Daniel's rifle grazed the former's ear.
Elliott then asked if Daniel was satisfied, but the
latter replied that he was not, and insisted on an-
other shot, this in spite of the entreaties of the two
seconds. The attitude of Elliott now changed, and
turning to Daniels he in substance said 'Sir, for the
gross insult which you have inflicted on my honor, I
have given you an opportunity to take my life, and
I had hoped that you would be satisfied; but since
you demand my blood, I now warn you that at the
next fire it is my purpose to kill you.' At the sig-
nal both men fired—Daniels missed, but Elliott's
ball passed through the former's heart causing in-
stant death. This Mr. Elliot was the half uncle
of Theodore Roosevelt, and....married my aunt,
Miss Lucy Sorrel." (The spelling and punc-
tuation are Mackall's.)

It is unlikely that this incident, even though their son
was involved, would have elevated Mr. Elliot in the opinion of Lucy's parents. The duel took place at a time in
Savannah when citizens were lobbying for legislation that

would make dueling grounds for murder charges, and this opinion was reflected by Charles Colcock, Jr., a contemporary of Lucy and her brothers who writes in a letter to his parents in the family's collection of letters *Children of Pride*:

> *"Miss Lucy Sorrel on tomorrow evening expects to espouse the name of Elliot. I wish her joy, but fear a disappointment. Were I a lady, I would certainly be very loath to marry one who had the guilt of homicide upon his skirts. The marriage is not, I am told, very warmly approved by her parents."*
> (p. 418)

In that same collection, Colcock's cousin Laura writes his sister of the town gossip on the subject.

> *"Mr. Stoddard informed Mr. Hutchison the other day that 'Lucy Sorrel would marry any man as rich as he was.' It seems that Miss Stoddard and Miss Sorrel are rival singers, and it is 'diamond cut diamond' with them just now..."* (p. 214)

Lucy's parents must have become reconciled to the idea of having Elliott for a son-in-law because the couple was married in their home on Harris Street by Dr. I.S.K. Axson, pastor of the Independent Presbyterian Church and friend of the family. Colcock's prediction that the marriage would prove a disappointment to Lucy came true, but not for the reasons he and others would have foretold. Lucy's love affair ended in tragedy when her husband of four short years died of pulmonary disease on August 3, 1862, leaving her with two young children, John Stewart and Matilda Moxley (Maude), the later named after Lucy's mother who had taken her own life six months before the birth of the child.

Lucy Ireland Sorrel Elliot lived almost forty more years. She spent her time traveling, participating in charitable works, singing in public concerts, and living at times with family in Virginia and Savannah. During the War Between the States, she personally helped supply her brothers' needs by sending them articles of clothing and other necessities. Records show that she, too, was one of the founding members of The Ladies Gunboat Association of which Francis was a benefactor. Though she remained socially active for many years to come, Lucy never remarried. Apparently Charles Green's words to her grandmother two years before her marriage were true, *"she loved the man intensely."* She died at the age of 72 on July 3, 1903 in Washington, D.C., but her body was returned to Savannah to be buried in the Laurel Grove Cemetery in the vault with her parents and her brother Moxley. It is unfortunate that a woman's life, marked with beauty, talent, adventure, devotion to family, and charity, would best be remembered by it's association with one of the last duels fought in Savannah.

Rodolphine Claxton Sorrel &
George Wayne Anderson Sorrel

Just a little over a year after Lucy's birth, the Sorrel's welcomed another girl who they christened Rodolphine Claxton after Francis' cousin and former love interest. She was born on September 16, 1832 in Savannah, but her life was short. Family records differ on the date of her death. One record states she died in August of 1833. She was alive in June of 1833 when Mrs. Claxton sent kisses to her namesake in a letter to the Sorrels. Another record indicates she died at the age of two, which would have been in 1834, the same year her younger brother George Wayne Anderson was born. George was named after Francis' friend and business partner G. W. Anderson, who was the president of Planter's Bank for many years. The young son was born July 7 in Prince William County, Virginia, probably at the home of Matilda's mother Aminta Moxley. He died in Springfield, Georgia. One record lists his death as 1834; another claims he lived a few years. The earlier death is more likely because there should have been more information regarding his life had he lived a few years. The cause for either child's death is unrecorded, but the loss of two children so close together would surely have strained Matilda's delicate mental state.

Gilbert Moxley Sorrel

The most famous of the Sorrel children was Gilbert Moxley Sorrel, the fourth child of Matilda and Francis. Handwritten Sorrel family notes indicate that he was born on February 23, 1837, a date that corresponds with the date of his recorded baptism in June of 1837, but history books, including the one he himself wrote, record his birth as 1838 as does the marker at his grave site. However, Moxley himself was dead before the publishing of his book, and both par-

**Moxley Sorrel,
Beginning of Civil War**

ents preceded him in death, so it is conceivable that his wife could have been mistaken. Too, a sister was born in December of 1834, what would be just ten months after Moxley if he were born in 1838. He was named after his maternal grandfather Gilbert Moxley and went by the middle name Moxley throughout his life.

Born about the time the Sorrels moved into the house

on the corner of Bull and Harris, Moxley grew up there and later lived in the dwelling next door that his father built to house the older sons of the expanding family. Directly across Bull street from the home they called *Shady Corner* was the Oglethorpe Barracks for the Georgia Militia where both Moxley and his younger brother Claxton mustered into the Georgia Hussars when the War Between the States became a possibility. It is no wonder that Moxley loved all things military. He grew up on a daily dose of military drills and parades right on his doorstep. Too, he had the examples of his brother-in-law William Whann Mackall, Aminta's husband, and his own brother Frank to emulate. He was an active outdoors man from an early age. In southern society, sporting events such as boating, hunting, horsemanship, archery, and the like gave young gentlemen a chance to demonstrate their manly character to their elders and members of the fairer sex. There's evidence that Moxley participated enthusiastically in events that required skill and a competitive spirit. Moxley was a

Oglethorpe Barracks, Rear View

member of the Savannah Cricket Club in 1859 when the Savannah Republican reports that the 22-year-old merchant was the top scorer in a match with 22 runs and three catches.

Moxley received some training in military tactics and drill at the Chatham Academy he attended for a short time. He, unlike his older brothers, did not attend college. He had been a member of the Georgia Hussars, an elite volunteer cavalry unit, for a year or two by the outbreak of the Civil War. He was a junior clerk for the Central Railroad banking house, but on June 1, 1861, his Georgia Hussar unit was mustered in for a period of about thirty days at which time he saw two brief tours of duty, one at Skidaway Island and the other in the capture of Fort Pulaski. However, the Confederate Army failed to recognize his unit, so Moxley left his job and "slipped off" to Charleston to watch the South Carolina militia bombard Fort Sumter. Once there, he desperately wanted to become part of the fray, and utilizing an introduction provided by his father to his friend, Colonel Thomas Jordan, the all-powerful adjutant-general to General Beauregard, he became a volunteer aid on General James Longstreet's staff and finally got a taste of battle. Apparently Longstreet was quite impressed with the young Moxley, and he quickly moved up the ranks first to captain and acting adjutant-general on Longstreet's staff, then to Major, to Lt. Colonel, and finally to Brigadier General in 1864. During his military career, Moxley was wounded twice, once resulting in an obituary in the New York Herald and news of his death circulating in Savannah. The first wound was minor, but the second pierced his lung with a bullet, and he went to his brother Frank for medical attention. While there, he acted as best man in Frank's wedding. Returning to duty after convalescing from this injury, he received news that Lee had surrendered. He and his brother Frank were paroled as POW's at Lynchburg and then made their way to Richmond where they took the loyalty oath to the United States of America. In May of 1865, General James Longstreet wrote thanking him for his service and commending him as a soldier and an officer of the Confederate Army.

> *"For more than three years you have performed in the most satisfactory manner the duties of Adj't Genl. of my Command. This was no sinecure position, but one which required the greatest amount of intelligence and energy both of which qualities you possessed in the highest degree."* (Thomas Jewett Goree Letters, Volume 1, The Civil War Correspondence, Family History Foundation)

After the war, Moxley returned to Savannah where he married Catherine (Kate) Amelie DuBignon on November 14, 1867, a young woman who was about ten years younger than he. He served on the city council, acted as vice president of the Georgia Historical

Society, chairman of the board of managers for the Telfair Academy, and manager of the Ocean Steamship Company. In 1870, Francis writes to his son Frank that Moxley and his brother Claxton *"are making a living in their business,"* the Sorrel Brothers' Shipping, Commission & Forwarding Merchants. The business must not have been a success because Moxley's net worth at about that time was listed at just $205.30. He moved from Savannah to New York to manage the steamship company's office there. He moved back to Savannah in 1894 and became the manager of the Georgia Export and Import Company, but he soon became ill and moved to Ronoake, Virginia, to be close to his brother and doctor Frank Sorrel.

With Moxley's health failing, his wife Kate encouraged him to write his memoirs of the war. Being a member of the Georgia Historical Society, Moxley believed that preserving history was vital and regretted not keeping a more detailed diary of his experiences in the war. He wrote *Recollections of a Confederate Staff Officer* from memory, and though he makes no attempt to describe the battles he fought in detail, the result is considered by many to be one of the best first-hand accounts of the Civil War in existence, the account especially noted for its personal character sketches and physical descriptions of most of the major southern players in the war: Beauregard, JEB Stuart, J. E. Johnston, Stonewall Jackson, D.H. Hill, A.P. Hill, Ewell, Early, Anderson, Mahone, Van Dorn, Polk, Brady, Bartow, Lamar. He fought in many major battles: Manassas (Bull Run), Seven Pines, Seven Day's battles, Second Manassas, Sharpsburg (Antietam), Fredricksburg, Gettysburg (where he had his horse shot and killed beneath him), Chickamauga, the Wilderness, Spotsylvania, Cold Harbor, and the siege of Petersburg. His close association with Longstreet who was Lee's second in command allowed him to associate freely with General Lee, a man he respected greatly and liked personally.

John W. Daniel in an introduction to Moxley's book writes of him:

> *"tall, slender, and graceful, with a keen dark eye, a trim military figure and an engaging countenance, he was a dashing and fearless rider, and he attracted attention in march and battle by constant devotion to his duties as adjutant general and became as well known as any of his commanders."*

The book *Virginians at War: The Civil War Experiences of Seven Young Confederates,* further describes Moxley as seen through the eyes of a woman hosting a party for Moxley's superior:

> *"a somewhat dour Lucy Buck plays hostess to General James Longstreet and his staff,"* and calls then Major Moxley Sorrel and fellow officer Major Thomas Walton her 'ideal of the chivalrous

knights of yore, so courteous and delicate in their manner.' " (p. 98)

An early picture of Moxley shows him to be a young, eager recruit, proud to be in uniform and ready to face any challenge. A later picture on display in the Georgia Historical Society shows him to be the tired, seasoned soldier wearied by the deprivations and ugliness of war.

No doubt his mother, had she lived, would have been pleased with the man her son became, and his Father Francis spoke highly of him always and placed much confidence in him and his brother Claxton. Moxley and Claxton were executors of his will, and letters written by Francis speak of Moxley visiting him often and helping in his care up to his death in 1870.

Moxley and his wife Kate were living with his brother Frank at his estate *The Barrens* in Roanoke, Virginia when he died at midnight on August 10, 1901 at the age of 64. His body was returned to Savannah to be buried in his parents' vault at the Laurel Grove Cemetery. Like Frank, Moxley left no surviving children.

Field Marshall Viscount Wolseley, as a young officer in the British Army, had been a military observer attached to Longstreet's staff. It was there that he met Moxley and grew to admire him. After Moxley's death, Field Marshall Viscount Wolseley writes to his wife Kate,

"Fortunate indeed is the man who like General Sorrel is entitled to remind those around his death-bed that he did his best to do his duty and to serve his country with heart and soul. The records of his life tell us how well, how faithfully he did serve her, and if anything can console you and others for his loss, it must be that."

To many, Gilbert Moxley Sorrel was and is the epitome of a southern gentleman and a good, confederate soldier.

Picture of Moxley from
Recollections from a Confederate Staff Officer

Matilda Ann Sorrel

Francis and Matilda named their next child Matilda Ann, born December 29, 1838, after her mother. She lived just six years dying on July 16 or June 16 (once again there's a discrepancy in records) in 1844. Baptism records show she was baptized in the Independent Presbyterian Church on April 21, 1839.

Her mother Matilda was 38 at the time of her death; Francis was 51. The senior Matilda had given birth to another child, Agnes, three months before the young Matilda died. Though the Sorrels had lost two previous children, the child Matilda was older than the first two had been at the times of their deaths, so her loss was greatly felt, most likely bringing on a period of despondency in her mother. Her sister Aminta notes that Matilda was *"a most pious child."*

Alexander Claxton Sorrel

Francis and Matilda named their final son born on August 17, 1840, after Alexander Claxton, the husband of Francis' cousin Rodolphine. Likewise, Alexander Claxton named his first son Francis Sorrel Claxton in honor of Francis.

Claxton Sorrel

Like his older brothers, Alexander Claxton Sorrel, would serve with distinction in the War Between the States. He, like Moxley, was a member of the Georgia Hussars and mustered into the army at the same time as Moxley and followed him to Virginia in 1861. Unlike Moxley, Claxton had a hard time acquiring a commission and remained a private for some time. Aminta's husband William wrote his wife that *"I have not been able to put Claxton on any active service. He came late and knew very few of the officers and few knew him. He will be more useful by August."* (William Whann Mackall Papers, Southern Historical Collection, University of North Carolina at Chapel Hill.)

Moxley writes in his *Recollections of a Confederate Staff*

Officer verifying that his brother did finally get a commission :

> *"My brother Claxton, my junior, was a fine, well set up young fellow and eager for the fray. He was also a private in the Hussars, and like myself had not waited for the company, but came on to Richmond. Here he fell in with some young Georgians from Athens, the Troop Artillery, a six-gun battery under command of Captain Carlton. Claxton joined and became a good artillerist and was a corporal when transferred. The First Georgia Regulars.... Its drill and discipline were supposed to be severer than that of other troops....was brought to Virginia and assigned to G. T. Anderson's Georgia Brigade."* (p. 46)

In 1862, Charles Colcock Jones, Jr. reports that Claxton Sorrel was killed in battle of Sharpesburg (*Children of Pride*, p. 244), but that obviously proved to be untrue. It is true that Claxton saw lots of battle. Correspondence between Francis and Claxton, nicknamed Clacky, reveals the struggles he encountered while trying to gain a commission in the Confederate Army. His father writes him, *"You are not, I trust, doomed to continual disappointments."*

Even though Claxton had his brothers Dr. Frank Sorrel and Moxley along with his brother-in-law William Mackall working behind the scenes for him, it wasn't until April of 1864 that Claxton received news that he had been given the rank of Captain in December of the previous year. Moxley states that he gave Claxton temporary detail on the staff of Brigadier-General Garnett and that Claxton was also appointed captain in the assistant Adjutant-General's Department and served with General John Bratton (*Recollections*, p. 46). Claxton's sisters and father worked throughout the war to keep him in the necessities of clothing and equipment, so though both he and his brother Moxley saw active battle and both suffered the deprivations of war, it is likely that Claxton's experiences were less privileged and even more bleak than those of Moxley.

Claxton returned to Savannah after the war and worked for a time with his brother to try to make a living with a company they called Sorrel Brothers' Shipping, Commission & Forwarding Merchants. On December 10,1867, he married Matilda Brent Hunton in Fauquier County, Virginia the month after Moxley wed Kate. Matilda Hunton

Matilda Hunton Sorrel

was most likely related to the Sorrel children on their mother's side, and it is obvious from letters that she was a friend to and in the company of Claxton's sisters Annie and Agnes in Virginia before they married. Francis, in a letter to his youngest daughter Annie, reports that Douglass' son Douglass, Jr. is living with Claxton and Matilda in 1868 while attending school in Savannah, and that Matilda is already showing signs of delicate health. In March of 1870, Francis writes Frank, Jr. that Claxton's wife, "*sweet woman, is an invalid and I fear will continue so to the end. Dear Claxton is kept in a constant state of anxiety. He is a devoted and kind husband.*"

This "invalid" state must have been due only to his wife's pregnancy, for she gave birth to their first child in September of that year, a child who died in the same month.

Letters reveal that Claxton, like Moxley and Francis' daughters, stayed with him often in Savannah until Francis' death in 1870. He, also like Moxley, was named an executor of his father's will.

On October 7, 1871, Claxton and Matilda had a son whom they named Francis. Claxton moved to Griffin, Georgia in 1872 to continue a career in the commission business as a cotton broker and a clerk in the C & S Bank. He and Matilda had five more children: John B. Hunton born in 1873 and died before his first birthday in 1874, Mary Foster who was born that same year but lived only five days, Gilbert Moxley born in March of 1876 and lived to adulthood, another unnamed child who was born and died on September 1, 1878, and Agnes who was born on November 14, 1879.

Though Claxton seemed to be destined to walk in the footsteps of his older and always popular brother Moxley, he appeared not to resent it; he named a son after him.

Like his older half brother Douglass, Claxton struggled with finances. He and Moxley failed in a business endeavor, and a claim against Francis' estate in 1879 indicates Claxton had owed his sister-in-law Martha (Douglass' wife) and her heirs $1250 since 1869 and could not pay it because he *"is now and has been for four or 5 years insolvent."* Claxton died at the age of 68 on January 10, 1908 in Griffin-Spalding, Georgia a year before his wife Matilda died.

Agnes Eugénie Sorrel

Francis and Matilda's seventh child was born March 11, 1844, at 6 A.M., just three months before they lost their six-year-old daughter Matilda. Her name is one of the few clues to the identity of Francis's mother. Due to the fact that the Sorrels had given their previous children the full names of the people for whom they were named, Agnes

Agnes Sorrel Stoddard

Eugenie was probably the full name of Francis's mother. She is one of the younger sisters whom Moxley writes about in *Recollections of a Confederate Staff Officer*. She was seventeen years old at the outbreak of the Civil War in 1861, and she was the only member of the Sorrel family to lose a loved one in the war. She was betrothed to Edward Willis, a young man who lived across Madison Square from her family. Edward, called Ned by his friends, was the son of local prominent physician Francis Willis, and third in his senior class of fifty-six at West Point in 1861. He was made brigadier general by 1864, though he would never know it. Ned fought under General Stonewall Jackson, and was singled out for special praise on Jackson's death-bed. He was mortally wounded at the Battle of Bethesda Church, near Petersburg, and as he was dying, he sent word to Moxley to tell his sister of his death. He told a comrade,

"I am not afraid to die. I don't mind it myself, but it will break her heart and my poor father's and mother's. Tell her not to be distressed. I die in the best cause a man could fall in." (letter from Sandy Pendleton to Willis' father)

Moxley was summoned, and he wrote in *Recollections,*

"Our position was at some distance, but I was immediately sent for. Our families had long been neighbors in Savannah, and young Willis was soon to be one of us by a still closer tie. I was quickly by his side. He died on my arm, but not before whispering loving messages for home and to that one he bore on his brave heart to its last beat. The remains of this brilliant young soldier were sent home, accompanied by a guard of honor picked from the brigade by his division commander." (p. 260)

He died the day before his commission as brigadier general, signed by General Robert E. Lee, arrived. Ned died at the age of twenty-three, the youngest Confederate general in the field. Ned is just one example of the tragic waste of young ability and giftedness in the War Between the States. The official historian of the Twelfth Georgia Regiment wrote,

> *"He was cut down in the vigor of young manhood, when higher and brighter honors awaited him in his brilliant and promising career. On the threshold of renown, his pure, gentle and brave spirit was still, and the life of one of the brightest and most promising young officers in the Confederate army was closed forever...No hardships were too severe if borne for his beloved Country.* (Remarks by Michael Willis at Laurel Grove Cemetery, Savannah, Georgia, April 23, 1995)

Though there is a memorial stone for him beside the Sorrel vault in the Laurel Grove Cemetery in Savannah (it was placed there long after the Civil War), he may be buried elsewhere; his body was possibly re-interred after the Civil War by his father who had been a member of the Confederate Medical Corps.

Though young Ned sacrificed his life for what he thought was a most noble cause, Agnes, like many fiancés and wives of that time, sacrificed a life as well, one that she would never know to be better or worse than the one that followed his loss. His death, and eventually hers, left questions that will never be answered. Did Agnes ever get over this first love, probably romantically left perfect in her mind by its abrupt and heroic termination? Did she pragmatically move on, or did Agnes forever compare the future she lived to the one she might have lived? At the young age of twenty, Agnes Sorrel had lost two of the most important people in her life to tragedy, her mother to suicide and her betrothed to war.

Pragmatically or not, Agnes moved on. She married John Irvine Stoddard three years later on May 16, 1867, at the age of twenty-three in the Independent Presbyterian Church in Savannah. Once again, the well-known Doctor I.S.K. Axson presided over the ceremony. Much is known about the husband Agnes was not to have; little is known about the one she had. A wealthy planter named John Stoddard (1809-1879) lived in Savannah and was an elder of the Independent Presbyterian Church (*Children of Pride*, p. 1694), as was Francis Sorrel. John Irvine Stoddard could have been his son, and if not his son, closely related to him. The young couple would have known each other as they attended the same church and their fathers were colleagues. Agnes' John may very well be the Mr. Stoddard quoted as gossiping about Agnes' sister Lucy in *Children of Pride*. (p. 214)

If John Irvine were the son of the planter John Stoddard, Agnes married well by the standards of Savannah society, but the younger John would have inherited a standard against which most young, southern men would not have wanted to be compared, that of the Civil War hero Ned Willis. However, Agnes writes to her brother-in-law Paul in 1896, *"there is no other love like that of husband & wife,"* so it appears that Agnes had not lost the chance to find true love and was happy in her relationship with her husband. They had four children, Matilda, (named after her then deceased mother) who died in infancy, Isabella who lived to old age, Francis who lived to adulthood and had three children of his own, and Irvine who died in childhood. Her first two children were born in Savannah, so she obviously lived close to her father until his death in 1870. Agnes died while living in Washington, DC, on June 19, 1898 at the age of fifty-four, ironically the same age her mother Matilda had died. Her body was returned to Savannah to be buried in Bonaventure Cemetery.

Annie Middleton Sorrel

Annie Sorrel Blech

Annie was the last child born to Francis and Matilda Sorrel. Matilda was forty at the time of her birth, Francis fifty-three. She was named after her great-grandmother on her mother's side, Anna Middleton Douglass. Born on August 31, 1846 at the Sorrel House at # 6 Harris Street, Annie was just thirteen when her mother plunged to her death. In a letter to his daughter on her twenty-second birthday while she was summering in Newport, Francis provides an account of her birth and evidence of his tenderness for his youngest child.

"I was sitting outside of my dressing room in the house, then mine, and now owned by Mr. Weed, overwhelmed with anxieties in regard to an event looked for to occur very soon. A beloved one was suffering within—my earnest prayers for her speedy relief were heard in Heaven, and it was not long before the cry of an infant who had just entered into this world made me joyous & thankful. In

due time I was invited to go in to congratulate my beloved wife for the mercies of God, and see the babe lying quietly at her side—that Babe was you, my dear Annie! ....And although we have been severely afflicted by the death of one of your parents, one is still left to you, who never expected to live to see you a woman."

Francis closes the letter with *"if you love me only half as much as I do love and cherish you, I shall be grateful if not satisfied."*

Other letters to Annie and family members reveal that Francis' home was still hers until his death. Though she married late, she obviously enjoyed an active social life, often in the company of her older, widowed sister Lucy Sorrel Elliot. In his later years, Francis complained they were often out late at night during the social season and he was left alone to miss them and his other children. Both young women were known for their beautiful singing voices and participated in concerts and the Savannah social scene.

Annie was the only unmarried child left at home when her father died in 1870, and it appears she was still single at that time because her father had been reluctant to let her go. She didn't marry until 1876 at the age of thirty. Her courtship and marriage, told of by her daughter Alice Sorrel Blech Wainwright in the Wainwright Genealogy makes for a very romantic story.

Paul Adolph Eduard Blech was born in Danzig,

Germany, the son of staunchly Lutheran parents. His grandfather was a Lutheran Bishop, and his father was the superintendent of a Lutheran College. Paul moved to England as a young man along with several other young men from his city, to make careers for themselves in the cotton industry because Danzig provided few economic opportunities. His job in an English export-import firm led him to Savannah, Georgia, in 1869 where he was among many of the young people who visited the Sorrel home that was known as a "rallying" place, of sorts, for young people. Paul was a conscientious young man and thought it best to have a plan for supporting Annie before formally "addressing" her. This was a wise move on his part, but apparently Francis, Annie's father, was unimpressed with the idea of Annie, his youngest, dearest, and only unmarried daughter, moving away, especially as far away as the young, foreign Mr. Blech was likely to take her. Paul's firm made the decision to send him to Alexandria, Egypt, as its representative because long staple cotton was also grown there. In anticipation of the move, Paul immediately wrote the twenty-three-year-old Annie and requested that she marry him and move with him to Alexandria. Annie, according to her daughter, was very much in love with Paul and wrote him a letter accepting his proposal, but it was inappropriate for young women of that time and place to visit the post office, and because of her father's disapproval, none of her brothers would mail the letter. Not to be thwarted so easily, Annie asked a young boy passing the house to take her letter, along with postage, to the post office. The dishonest boy kept the money and never posted the letter, resulting in what Annie and Paul would later call "seven years lost." Paul, not hearing from Annie, and Annie, not hearing from Paul, each assumed the other was no longer interested.

Several years later, Annie accompanied her widowed sister Lucy Elliot and her two children to Europe where they visited many places before arriving in Paris, France. It was completely by happenstance, or fate as some would say, that Paul, too, was in France and had just departed Paris when a fellow passenger mentioned meeting the charming Mrs. Elliot from Savannah, Georgia (apparently Lucy had lost none of her ability to captivate men), and upon questioning, told Paul that she was accompanied by her sister, Miss Sorrel. Paul promptly departed the train at the next station from which he returned to Paris and found Annie. They were delighted that neither had married, and Annie, no longer restricted by the wishes of her father or the interference of her brothers, married Paul on July 18, 1876 in Paris, France.

Annie and Paul lived the rest of their married life between Alexandria, Egypt and Karlesruhe, Germany. Annie became a Germanized American and gave birth to her two children abroad; her son Adolph Eduard Sorrel Blech was born in Alexandria, Egypt, and her daughter Alice Matilda Agnes Blech was born in Dresden, Germany because the British were at odds with the Egyptians at that time, and all women and children were asked to leave Egypt. The Blechs lived a most unusual life, at times together and at times apart. The children learned German, French, Italian, and Arabic but were not taught English until later in life because their parents wanted to retain one language with which they alone could communicate.

The Blechs apparently lived an affluent lifestyle while in Egypt. They socialized with the elite, lived in nice homes in which they were served by a governess, a cook, and other attendants. When the two children were six and eight, Annie took the children to Germany so they could receive a good education while Paul stayed in Alexandria to maintain his business. Annie spent six months of each year with the children and left them with others while she spent six months with her husband. The children spent much of their lives separated from either or both of their parents. Paul spent the summer with them every other year, and they would visit different places together, vacations they all enjoyed immensely. According to Alice, these years as a whole were unhappy times for both parents and children because of their separations. In 1896, Annie's sister Agnes writes , somewhat disapprovingly, to Paul from Washington, DC, where she was then living, regarding these separations and Paul's poor health.

> *"In a recent letter from Annie she was so sad and distressed at the parting from you and so anxious about your health...It is marvelous to me to think of*

*the sacrifices that you and Annie have made in these
past years for your children. I hope that Edward &
Alice will appreciate it & never forget that their parents gave up some of the best years of their intercourse
in life for their benefit…I think that Annie ought to
be with you now, for life is short at best & there is no
other love like that of husband & wife."*

Either from this illness or another, Annie's husband
Paul died in 1901 at the age of sixty-one, and Annie and
her daughter returned to the United States and settled
in Washington, D.C. Her son followed the next year and
changed his name from Adolph Eduard to Edward Sorrel
Blech, a move that was no doubt advantageous considering the anti-German sentiment and negative ramifications
to come of the name Adolph during his lifetime as a natu-
ralized citizen.

Apparently Annie and her children were not financially secure upon moving to the United States because
Annie's daughter got a job as a typist for Pan-American
Union. She later became a social secretary to Mrs. William
Howard Taft at the White House. She resigned that position in 1910 to marry a naval officer, Richard Wainwright,
Jr., and it was with the Wainwrights that Annie was living
in Virginia when she died on July 13, 1934, just shy of
her eighty-eighth birthday. She, too, had her remains returned to Savannah where she is buried in the family vault
at Laurel Grove Cemetery.

6

The Sorrels and Slavery

Francis Sorrel began life in a slave culture. His father's first wife owned plantations in St. Domin_gue, and the wealth that Antoine accumulated was made possible by the practice of slavery. If Francis' mother were a member of the *gens de couleur libres*, she too would most likely have owned slaves as would the relatives who raised him. After he moved to the United States, Francis and his most intimate friends and contacts were all slaveholders. He married two women who had grown up in a slave-holding family. Though Francis witnessed firsthand a civil war brought on by slavery, it is not surprising that he would become a slave owner himself. It would have been odd had he not. He moved to the antebellum South in which the pecking order was clearly defined. Those with prestige and wealth owned slaves, as did some free blacks. Francis was an ambitious man set on becoming a member of the upper crust, a goal he pursued systematically and diligently until it was achieved. Owning slaves was just one of the ways in which he attained his goal.

Francis' father Antoine from his new home in Louisiana sought his son's help in procuring slaves for the nephew of the cousin Jacque Joseph Sorrel who had given him a home. In a letter written in French to Francis in 1827, Antoine tells Francis that *"you will gratify me especially to have great confidence in him and his neighbors."* With this letter came a request for help in procuring *"20 to 30 slaves from 16 to 18 years of age, well built and of good behavior."*

The nephew, Francis' cousin Solange Sorrel, further lists the stipulations,

> *"I will want to know what will be the price of such slaves, what will be the steps that will be necessary to own them, if it would be better to buy them at Baltimore or in your State, and what will be the most favorable time. If it would be better to transport them at your place, my brother will make the trip, and you would be good to help him with your advice."*

On the blank page opposite Solange's signature on this letter there is the following faint notation in English that appears to be a draft of Francis' answer to Solange:

"If you particularly wish them of the age named say 16 to 18 it is believed they can be obtained more readily in Balto (Baltimore) or Charleston. Here such 400$ paid for them. From 16 to 30 years would be of the same value. By spending two to three months here....the number wanted might be obtained. Possibly in the course of one month they could be had. A few might be got for 325$ but character not warranted. The same person from whom I obtained my intelligence has an order for the purchase of 20 prime Negroes, male, from the age of 18 to 30, limited @ 350$ & no inquiries made be healthy. In families, they bring about 250 to 275$ sound."

By October of 1828, Solange had upped his request to *"50 or 60 slaves, large or small, but I want at least twenty or twenty-five men ready to work."* If Solange received these slaves, he did not use them long for he was shot from ambush as he crossed a bridge over Bayou Teche while walking home from an evening with his brother Marcial in 1835. Five of his own slaves were hanged for the crime. It would be interesting to know if these five were procured for him by Francis.

Francis not only helped others attain slaves, he owned slaves. Property tax records from 1826 record Francis as the owner of three slaves when he owned nothing else and before he married into the Moxley family, so he did not inherit the slaves or the practice of slavery from the women he married. Accurate and consistent slave records of that time and place are hard, if not impossible, to find, especially records of specific slaves. The individual identities of whole generations of enslaved black Americans are lost. At best, in most cases, there survive lists including age, sex, and identification of race as either *B* for black or *M* for mulatto with the name of the owner on that particular census. There appear to be only two such censuses in Savannah in the years before the Civil War, those of 1850 and 1860. Otherwise, there is documentation of the number of slaves owned by each person listed on existing property tax roles as a way for the government to tax owners on their net worth. In those documents, there is no mention of age or sex, but the owner is charged different amounts for slaves in regard to age, so some information can be ascertained through those records. Identities of specific slaves have most commonly been found in personal diaries, letters, indentures (business documents), bills of sale, wills, and in a few cases, the personal writings of the slaves themselves, the last being rare as it was illegal for slaves to read and write. The Sorrel family leaves little information by which to track the black members of their household, so it's hard to determine much about the people who helped rear the Sorrel children, cook their meals, clean their houses, and, in general, make possible the lavish, indulged lifestyles the Sorrels lived as members of the antebellum Savannah elite.

According to the existing property tax records found at the Georgia Archives in Morrow, Georgia, the Sorrels appeared to own very few slaves throughout the years. However, these numbers conflict with the 1850 and 1860 slave censuses also found in the Georgia Archives. In 1850, there are slaves under two lists for Francis Sorrel, one in his name only and one in that of Francis Sorrel Trustee. There is no evidence of a list similar to the latter in an 1860 census, but this does not necessarily mean that one did not exist. It may have been lost or not yet discovered.

Slave census of 1850 for Francis Sorrel:

> 70 year-old female, Black
> 40 year-old female, Black
> 45 year- old female, Black
> 35 year-old male, Black
> 19 year-old male, Black

Slave census of 1850 for Francis Sorrel Trustee:

> 22 year-old female, Mulatto
> 25 year-old female, Mulatto
> 35 year-old female, Mulatto
> 10 year-old female, Mulatto
> 9 year-old female, Mulatto
> 8 year-old female, Mulatto

3 year-old male, Mulatto
9 year-old male, Mulatto

Slave Census of 1860 for Francis Sorrel:

80 year-old female, Black
50 year-old female, Black
30 year-old male Black
27 year-old Male, Black
12 year-old Male, Black
19 year-old, Male, Mulatto
30 year-old Male, Black
20 year-old Female, Mulatto

The 1850 census for Francis Sorrel Trustee is the first record of Francis Sorrel being associated with more than six slaves, and it is interesting to note that all are of mixed race whereas the slaves recorded under the name of Francis Sorrel are all listed as black. This information creates several questions. For whom was Francis holding these slaves in trust? Why were they not listed on property tax records? Where did they live, and in what way did they serve?

To answer the first question, one would assume the trust was for a female as women were not allowed to own property in their own names. Francis Sorrel was an astute businessman known to create trusts to safeguard his assets from loss or to attain the benefits associated with trusts. One such trust is the one in which he appointed his friend George W. Anderson as trustee for his wife Matilda and their children with which he made sure they were provided for if anything should happen to him. However, if the 1850 trust, too, was set up for his wife, wouldn't the slaves be listed under household property? This second group of people may have been used as servants for their business, and if so, they could have been considered a business expense and not personal property. Then again, there's the possibility that they were in trust for a friend. This is unlikely considering that what appears to be two of them, the 9-year-old male and the 10-year-old female, turn up ten years later under the list for Francis Sorrel. The 1860 census lists Francis as having more slaves, eight, than he has ever claimed before on property tax. This gives credence to the belief that Francis probably had more slaves all along, and they were not listed on personal property tax because he claimed them in another name or considered them as part of his business assets. They may have actually lived on site at the business, been rented out and lived with their renters, lived in the carriage house on Harris Street, or they may have been housed in a combination of these ways.

Another interesting aspect of the group of trustee slaves is that they are all mulattos. According to Walter J. Fraser, Jr. in his book *Savannah in the Old South* (University of Georgia Press, 2003) there were nearly 2000 mulattos in Savannah in 1860. He sees this number as a testimony of the master/slave sexual relationships that took place in the antebellum South; however, only 20% of all slaves in Savannah were mulattos. It is interesting to note that in the list of trustee mulatto slaves, there are no adult men, three women of child-bearing age, and the other five are children who one might reasonably assume are their children. Two of these children are retained in the household to be listed in the 1860 census.

Lack of information regarding this second group of mixed-race slaves creates many questions? What happened to the other women and children? It is unlikely that that many young people would have died over the ten-year period between the two censuses. Were they connected to Francis in some personal way, and did he grant them their freedom before 1860? Did he sell them?

Francis retired from business in the late 1850's. If they were slaves used in the business, they would no longer have been needed. Too, Francis had lived in the midst of one slave insurrection, and he may have clearly read the signs that the Civil War was imminent, choosing to begin to divest himself of slaves to forego the heavy financial losses incurred by many of his southern friends and neighbors by their emancipation. Francis Sorrel was still a wealthy man at the end of the war, so he may have further reduced his slave holdings between the time of the 1860 census and 1865 emancipation.

Unfortunately, very little information has come to light that could be used to track these black members of the Sorrel household. There are only a couple of slaves mentioned in family letters found as of yet. In a letter written in April of 1839 to Aminta at school, Francis writes,

> *"Moxley is on the floor cutting all manner of antics*
> *for the amusement of little Matilda, who is seated*
> *in old mammy's lap, enjoying the fun to the utmost*
> *of her powers."*

Mammy's real name is not given there or when she is again mentioned in a letter from Ireland, the family place in Virginia, in 1860 when Francis asks Claxton at home in Savannah to *"remember us to the servants, especially to old mammy"*. She is probably the 70-year-old listed in the 1850 slave census and again as an 80-year-old in the 1860 census. This may be the same woman as *"Old Nanny"* for whom Francis asks Annie to bring *"a couple of large handkerchief....bright colors"* in October of 1868. If so, Mammy was then 88 and liberated.

In that same letter, Francis writes, *"Moselle is as faithful as ever. Bring her a little present..."* She too may be a servant retained from slavery, but obviously the men he employed after the war were not. He continues to write, *"My men servants have annoyed me. I have had to change them several times."*

The property and census records indicate that Francis did not retain some of his slaves for long periods of time. Other than Mammy, the only slaves Francis mentions personally as wanting to keep are those listed in the trust of 1844 mentioned earlier. Slaves who were to be held in trust

for Matilda and children were *"Nancy and her son Andrew
and her daughter Judy and Judy's son William and Nancy."* Either
Francis mentions Nancy twice or there are two Nancy's, the
second possibly another child of Judy, granddaughter of
Nancy. Perhaps the first Nancy is the aged Mammy listed in
the censuses, Judy one of the younger middle-aged women,
and the younger slaves their children. Some of the slaves
may have died instead of being sold, but two of Francis'
indentures reveal that he sold Minda to R.W. Stiles in 1829
a few months before his first wife died, and in 1833 he sold
"Louisa, aged about 25, and her daughter Virginia about 10
months" to a William W. Gordon for $400.

All the slave information mentioned thus far pertains
to the slaves owned by the Sorrels in Georgia. The Sorrels
also owned the Ireland property in Virginia. Did they keep
another staff of servants to maintain the house and land
there, or did they take their slaves from Savannah with
them when they went to Virginia? There is the possibility
that Francis and Matilda owned slaves in Virginia as well
as Georgia.

Francis' support of slavery solidified his standing in
the community of Savannah. His southern friends and associates welcomed the man of like mindedness into their
midst, and in a letter to a friend from whom he rented
summer accommodations in Massachusetts, he reveals
that he is truly one of them in sentiment as well as practice. He writes,

"Great Barrington must be a great nest of rank

*abolitionists. How can you get along with those fa-
natics? But I suppose you keep them in the dark as
to the number of their nigger brothers you hold in
subjugation. If it should be known, I have no doubt,
they would drive you away from their midst."*

Francis revealed himself time and time again as a survivor. He was resilient and pragmatic, as his father had been. When Sherman took Savannah, Francis welcomed him as a neighbor, and he and his daughters attended parties at the home of Charles Green, Francis' close friend and nephew by marriage, whose house was Sherman's headquarters. Alexander A. Lawrence in "A Present for Mr. Lincoln" writes

*"Major Hitchcock describes a gay party at Sherman's
headquarters on the night of January 5 attended
by a number of prominent Savannahians, including Francis Sorrel, the father of General Moxley
Sorrel. The latter's sister was also present. While
the ladies did not disguise their sympathy, reported
Hitchcock they showed none of the 'vile rebel vin-
dictive spirit you find elsewhere. While his father
was fraternizing with Sherman and conceding that
the South's cause was utterly hopeless, Moxley
was recovering from a painful leg wound he had
recently received in Virginia. A few weeks later at
Hatcher's Run a bullet pierced his lung, breaking*

the ribs on both sides.' "(The Story of Savannah from Secession to Sherman, A. A. Lawrence, The Ardivan Press, Macon, 1961, p. 225)

Francis attended these parties before the Sorrel sons, fighting for the Confederate Army, had surrendered to the Union. There were those who thought that Francis was actually the impetus behind Charles Green's gracious offer of his home to Sherman as a wily way of warding off destruction and financial ruin for the citizens of Savannah.

A Group of Unidentified Slaves in Savannah

The Sorrel children were proponents of slavery, as was their father. Aminta and her husband owned and used slaves to run their Langley Plantation. Douglass was among an elite few who owned more than fifty slaves, and, according to family lore, at least two of his sons became members of the Ku Klux Klan after slavery was abolished. The military careers of Frank, Moxley, and Claxton reveal their support for the institution of slavery. Lucy was a member of committees that supported the Confederate War effort, and Agnes lost her fiancé in support of the cause. Slavery was abolished before Annie was old enough to show an allegiance, but there is no reason to believe that she would have felt or behaved any differently than her siblings. Francis Sorrel, the man whose own mother may have been of mixed race, gave birth to a whole new generation of those who believed in the supremacy of the white race. If they, too, were of mixed race, it's very unlikely that they knew it.

7

Extended Family/Friends of the Sorrels

Richard Henry Douglass

Richard Henry Douglass was a friend to Francis long before he was related to him by marriage. He was Aminta Douglass' younger brother, and it was through Richard Henry that Francis met both of his wives. Francis first met him and his brother George when they were doing business in Saint-Domin gue as sugar and coffee merchants. Richard sponsored Francis' move to America after the boy's own father had left him in Haiti to fend for himself. In a letter to his younger brother William in 1813, Richard writes,

"I am glad poor Sorrel is safe and clear of his devoted Country" and instructs him to *"Give my respects to Sorrel & assure him of my increasing friendship. I expect it might be more agreeable to*

him to put up at the French Coffee House."

The Coffee House to which Richard sent him turned out to be one owned and operated by Francis' own mother's sister, though neither Richard nor Francis knew it at the time. Richard also arranged for him to learn English before he started working for him in the States, and he then set him up as a partner in Savannah. Francis named his first child after Richard Henry, and letters from Francis to him express his admiration and gratitude.

Richard Henry Douglass married Letitia Grace McCurdy, the Scottish governess to his brother George's children, a marriage that caused a lifelong rift between the families of the two brothers. Richard died at the age of forty-eight the same year that Francis married his niece Matilda, and though Richard left instructions for his *"beloved brother George"* to act as guardian of his children and executor of his will if his young wife did not abide by the stipulations set forth in it, George refused the privilege of both. There is no evidence that the problems between the brothers affected either's relationship with Francis, and Richard remained close to his sister Aminta, Francis' mother-in-law, and his nieces and nephews until his death.

Rodolphine & Alexander Claxton

Rodolphine Laval was reportedly Francis' first cousin on his mother's side though he apparently knew nothing of her until he arrived in Baltimore and quite fortuitously found her mother and her running a boarding and coffee house. Richard Henry Douglass had chosen to send him there because the proprietors spoke French. One can only imagine both his and his relatives surprise when they realized the connection. Supposedly, the senior Mrs. Laval's husband had been guillotined in the French Revolution, and the Lavals were endeavoring to eke out an existence in their adopted country, America. Family records and folklore do not explain why Francis had lost contact with his aunt, if indeed she was his aunt, but they do indicate that

Rodolphine Laval & Alexander Claxton

Francis fell in love with his beautiful cousin and may have even helped her to better herself, but he lost out to the man she would later marry, Alexander Claxton, a young naval officer. Francis apparently did not hold a grudge. The two men became intimate friends with each naming a son after the other one. Francis and Matilda also named a daughter after Rodolphine. The two families communicated with each other for the remainder of their lives, and the Claxtons were guests of the Sorrels when in Savannah. Letters reveal Alexander to be a witty, fun-loving man, but he was also a well-known and highly regarded naval officer. The two men shared many acquaintances, and it appears that Francis introduced Alexander to many of his own friends on the east coast and in Savannah. Probably because of the nature of his work, Alexander seemed to have an obsession with life insurance policies and encouraged his friend Francis in more than one letter to acquire a policy for himself. Alexander's fears were realized when he died unexpectedly in June of 1841. At the time he was the commander of the Pacific Squadron, and his funeral in Baltimore was attended with much fanfare and a Naval escort. The World War II Destroyer Claxton was later named for Alexander and his brother who was killed in the Battle of Lake Erie in 1813.

The widow Rodolphine received a widow's pension beginning in 1846 and ending in 1863 when it was discovered from *"information from numerous and reliable sources"* that Rodolphine Claxton was *"a noted and avowed secessionist, giving her sympathy and influence, openly and decidedly to the cause of rebellion."* Rodolphine died in 1863, and despite the efforts of her heirs, Francis and Alexander, Jr., the U.S. Government adamantly refused to reconsider and allow them to receive benefits from their father's naval career. (Information taken from notes of Jarvis Freymann).

Charles Green

Charles Green

Charles Green is probably best known as the man who saved Savannah from destruction by offering his home to General William Tecumseh Sherman at the end of his famous March to the Sea. Charles was never an American citizen. Born in Hales-Owen, Shropshire, England, he became a cotton merchant and probably first met Francis Sorrel through the Moxley family in Greenwich, Virginia where Green's sister and his mother had either lived or spent a considerable amount of time.

Though Charles Green was a British subject and claimed that he had no allegiance in the Civil War, he was arrested and held in Ft. Warren at the same time General William Mackall was there. He was arrested for what his granddaughter called *"a trifling: smuggling in a pair of scarlet Russian boots."* In actuality, he may have been involved in the profitable trade of penetrating the Federal blockade of southern ports. Moxley Sorrel in *Recollections of a Confederate Staff Officer* tells of Green's stay in prison, an experience made uncomfortable only by the fact that Green was housed with his business partner and fellow Englishman, Andrew Low, another well-known, wealthy Savannah businessman.

> *"When General Mackall was exchanged out of Ft. Warren he told me of two other prisoners, civilians, Andrew Low & Charles Green. The later had married my cousin, and both were Englishmen of the regular holdfast, energetic type. They constituted the most important business house in Savannah, were making quantities of money, but had quarreled and were about separating on the worst terms, when Seward's detectives, suspicious of their movements (they had both married in Savannah and were truly Southern and Confederate) clapped them in Ft. Warren. There by the irony of fate, they were the sole occupants of the same casemate, these....friends, now bitter, nonspeaking enemies. The situation was difficult and rather enjoyed by some gentlemen outside who knew of the partner's troubles."* (p. 79)

Like Francis Sorrel, Charles Green survived the Civil War a wealthy man.

Little is known about Charles Green's first wife by whom he had at least one child, possibly three. Jarvis Freymann, great-great grandson of Francis, thinks Charles

Green and his first wife had three: Benjamin Burroughs Green, Charles Green, Jr., and Andrew Low Green.

As Green's second wife he married Lucinda Ireland Hunton, the daughter of Lucinda and Matilda Moxley Sorrel's sister, Anne Dent Moxley Hunton; therefore, Charles became Francis Sorrel's nephew by marriage. His wife was named after Francis' first wife. Charles and Francis became good friends, and their association is probably the reason Charles

Lucinda Hunton Green

Green chose Madison Square to build what is now known as the Green-Meldrim House on the corner of West Macon Street. The mansion, situated just across the street from the Sorrel homes, was one of the most elaborate houses, inside and out, ever constructed in Savannah. It was built in 1853 several years after the Sorrels built their mansion on the corner of Harris and Bull, and the children of both families were close as were their parents, in and out of one another's homes and very much involved in one another's lives.

It was in Green's house that General Sherman set up

his headquarters in 1864 at the end of his march. It was also in this house that Sherman wrote a letter to President Lincoln bestowing upon him the city of Savannah as a Christmas gift. Many attribute the saving of the city from fire and destruction to the diplomatic efforts of Charles Green. It is possible that Francis Sorrel, through his intimate relationship with Green, had a hand in saving the city, as well.

The two families traveled together, vacationed together, and had summer homes in Greenwich, Virginia adjacent to each other and to their mother-in-law at The Grove. The Lawn, the Green's place there, was probably part of the same parcel the Moxley daughters inherited from their father Gilbert.

Charles and Lucinda Hunton Green, had seven children before she simply *"faded away,"* as her daughter put it. Lucy had been a *"gentle, firm Prince William County girl...who*

Home of Charles Green,
Sherman's Headquarters While in Savannah

bore him many children and faded away....He (Charles) had a firm hand with his first two wives, effectually reducing their healths & spirits..." (*All My Love*, Ann Green, notes from Freymann Genealogy)

Green's granddaughter further describes him in a book she wrote as *"a handsome gentleman with deep blue eyes, a florid complexion, a taste for elegant dress & surroundings. He also owned much cotton, had an unholy passion for banking..."* (*With Much Love*, notes from Freymann Genealogy)

Sixty at the time of his wife's death, Charles was to marry a third time. He married yet another of Mrs. Moxley's granddaughters and her namesake, as well, Aminta Elizabeth Fisher, the daughter of Sophia Mary Moxley Fisher. Apparently, in the much younger Aminta he had met his match.

> *"Nemesis came to him with a boomerang when he laid his heart & fortune at the feet of Miss Aminta Elizabeth Fisher of Baltimore....She thwarted the nice old bully's love of magnificence, sending the contents of his cellars to hospitals, rare brandies to paupers' wards, reducing his expenses, cutting down entertainment."* (All My Love, Ann Green)

Charles and Aminta had one daughter who died young. Aminta established an orphan home in Savannah, The Minnie Mission House, in their daughter's honor (she too was named Aminta). His third wife outlived him. He died in 1881, ten years after the death of his good friend and uncle by marriage, Francis Sorrel. The two families were further united when Charles' daughter Anne married William and Aminta Mackall's son William Whann, Jr. (Francis' grandson), and the two of them inherited the Lawn upon Charles' death, keeping in the family the land inherited from their mutual ancestor Gilbert Moxley.

8

A Tight Network

Richard Henry Douglass, the Claxtons, and Charles Green were related to the Sorrels as well as being their good friends. The Fishers in Baltimore were another example of relations who were good friends. Lucinda and Matilda Sorrel's youngest sister Sophia Mary Parham Moxley married an attorney, James Isom Fisher of Baltimore, and the Sorrels, parents and children, stayed with them when visiting there. The Claxtons were introduced to the Fishers by the Sorrels, and they, too, became friends. It was the Fisher's daughter who became Charles Green's third wife. The Sorrels enjoyed a tight network of family and friends who intermarried, socialized, and did business together.

George W. Anderson was another good friend of the Sorrels. He was the president of Planter's Bank, a plantation owner, and a business partner of Francis at one time. He, Charles Green, and Francis, along with their families, all attended and were influential members of the Independent Presbyterian Church under the leadership of the well-known pastor I.S.K. Axsom, a man who also became a close friend to Francis.

The Axsom family dined with the family and stayed with them in their Virginia home. Their daughter Ellen who later became Woodrow Wilson's first wife was a friend of Annie Sorrel. Francis well knew the benefit of knowing the right people and being known by them. Though he was surely viewed as an outsider when he first arrived on the Savannah scene, he made a place for himself and his family among those considered by anyone there to be the best of Savannah society. He counted amongst his friends the names Habersham, Telfair, Elliot, Jones, Law, Cohen, Low, Stoddard...the people who built Savannah and made it the city is today. The Creole youth named Mathurin François Sorrel had come far from his Haitian roots.

9

The Sorrel Homes

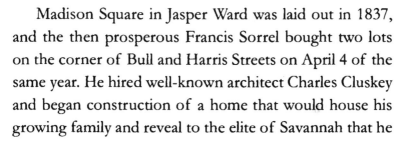

Madison Square in Jasper Ward was laid out in 1837, and the then prosperous Francis Sorrel bought two lots on the corner of Bull and Harris Streets on April 4 of the same year. He hired well-known architect Charles Cluskey and began construction of a home that would house his growing family and reveal to the elite of Savannah that he

**The Sorrel Mansion on the corner of Harris & Bull Streets.
The family called it *Shady Corner*.**

had indeed taken advantage of the boon period that the town had experienced in the '30's. The Sorrel House, the home the Sorrels called *Shady Corner*, was and still is a wonderful example of the luxuriant homes built in Savannah by wealthy planters and merchants during the South's prosperous antebellum period. The architect combined popular local elements with a "double-pile plan," a layout in which a room at the

Front Entry Hall of Sorrel Mansion on the Corner of Bull and Harris

front of the house is matched by a room at the rear creating a house two rooms thick on the main floors. The house consists of a full basement, two main floors, and an attic.

The rooms on the first floor are entered through a columned portico accessed by matching stairways separated by a street-level basement entry. Double doors lead to a wide center passage with a vestibule denoted by columns matching those on the portico. Adhering to the symmetry of the Greek Revival style, the house is separated down the middle by a spacious passageway with two large rooms on either side. To the left are double parlors of equal size, both thought to have been used for formal entertaining for which the Sorrels were well known. Linked by large mahogany pocket doors, the two rooms served as a venue for dancing, dining, and when necessary, separate quarters for male and female socializing. These rooms have lofty ceilings topped by decorative egg and dart plaster work and ornate medallions that once set off gas-lit chandeliers that showed to advantage the lavish furnishings, floor-length windows with gilded cornices, and coal-burning fireplaces of black

Egyptian marble below ornate gilded mirrors. It's not hard to imagine the rooms crowded with fashionable Savannahians in period attire treading upon the plush Brussels-carpeted heart pine floors.

Formal Parlor of Sorrel Mansion on Corner of Bull and Harris

To the right of the foyer is a large, less formal family parlor, backed by the family dining room, both accessed by a stairway between the two rooms that ascends from the kitchens on the bottom floor and, at one time, continued to spiral upward to the floors above. The dining room is smaller than the other rooms, but is unique in that it has curved walls and arched doors.

A long service corridor designed for easy access to two separate kitchens and the back yard, stable, and carriage house separated the basement of the Sorrel House at one time. Upon entering from the street level, the kitchen on the right has two fireplaces along the far wall that were used to prepare meals to be taken upstairs by the dumb waiter on that level or by servants using the circular stairs that ran from the basement all the way to the attic. To the left of the corridor was a second kitchen with a fireplace thought to be used for the preparation of meals for the house slaves who lived predominantly above the stables in the detached carriage house. There was also room in the basement for servants' quarters, probably those of the cook or possibly a house servant or two.

When the Sorrels moved into the house on Harris and Bull, there were five children ranging in ages from one to fifteen, two adults, and at least five slaves living there. Assuming the slaves lived in the carriage house or in the basement, there remained seven people to be housed in the four bedrooms on the second floor. As more children came along, it appears that the attic was utilized as well. The third floor was divided into four bedrooms, each with a fireplace and window, with a central hall-like room probably used for a nurse to be in attendance throughout the night.

The two main floors of the house are surrounded on three sides by spacious porches. These floors were accessed through floor-length windows that opened to them and expanded the living and entertaining space for most of the year in Savannah. These large, door-like windows also allowed for breezes to circulate throughout the house for all but about three months of the year in Savannah.

The two back corners of the house have large, closet-like rooms that made it possible for the servants to enter each room from the outside without going through the central rooms.

The Sorrel mansion was one of which the Sorrels were surely proud, especially Francis who had overcome so much hardship. It was an affluent location from which the family could walk to their church, The Independent Presbyterian Church, and Francis, and later his sons, could conduct his business on the bay. The Green, as Madison Square was then called, was used by all, and letters document its communal use for picnics, outings, parades, drills, and outings of all kind.

Daughters Aminta and Lucinda were married in the parlor at Shady Corner, and, Moxley in his *Recollections of a Confederate Staff Officer* tells of a visit to his family home by Robert E. Lee. The inventory of the house set forth in a trust that Francis had drawn up for his wife and children shows that the house was furnished lavishly and in a way to accommodate a large number of guests. The 1844 inventory included the following, among other items:

> 6 dozen silver forks and spoons
> 1 silver teapot
> 4 dozen tea and dessert spoons
> 1 silver coffee pot
> 1 silver ladle & fish knife

1 silver pitcher
1 large felt dining table
2 mahogany dining tables
4 mahogany wardrobes
3 mahogany toilets
3 mahogany and marble washstands
3 mahogany bedsteads
8 beds
4 couches
2 sofas
2 dozen mahogany chairs
3 arm chairs
4 Brussells carpets
1 hearth table
4 astral lamps
Kitchen dishes and furniture

An 1850 census shows all eight children still living in Savannah in the house on the corner of Bull and Harris. Even Aminta who was married and listed as a resident of Virginia was with them as were twenty-five-year-old Douglass and twenty-four-year-old Frank. Other relatives and

friends often were in residence there for long periods of time. It is no wonder that Francis felt the need for more space; in 1856, he had another three-story home complete with additional carriage house built on the remainder of the extra lot that he had originally purchased, and there his sons, including twenty-year-old Moxley and eighteen-year-old Claxton, took up residence.

On June 14, 1859, Francis and Matilda sold the mansion on the corner to Henry D. Weed for the sum of $23,000. This is the same year that Francis built Sorrel Block, and that expense may have had something to do with the selling of the mansion he and his wife had built.

An 1860 census taken after the death of Matilda shows Francis, Moxley, Claxton, Agnes, and Annie living in the house at #12 Harris. It is ironic that Francis and Matilda's married life ended with the selling of the house on the corner.

Francis lived in the house at #12 Harris until his death in 1870. Francis' comfortable lifestyle did not seem to be altered much by the Civil War. He was still considered a wealthy man, and in a letter to his daughter Annie in 1868 he still writes of two female servants and men servants, the latter of which were an annoyance to him. Annie had selected new carpets for him in New York, and he was entertaining several family members in his home as well as paying for Annie to travel. He left a sizeable estate when he died two years later.

The home at # 12 Harris was sold in 1871 for $14,500

to John W. Beckwith, the Episcopal bishop of Savannah. The house was separated from the Episcopal church by the house of Charles Green on the corner across Harris Street; therefore, #12 Harris Street may have been the manse for the church from 1871 to 1882. In 1882, the property at #12 Harris street was deeded to Kate A Dubignon Sorrel, wife of Moxley, and they kept the house until after Moxley's death. Moxley's wife deeded the property to Aminta Sorrel's son William W. Mackall, Jr. in 1903. William lived in Savannah and practiced law there, and his name is on legal documents pertaining to the Sorrels. He kept the home until 1919 when it was once again sold out of the family.

10

Charles B. Cluskey, Architect

Charles B. Cluskey is widely accepted as the architect of the Sorrel House, now called the Sorrel-Weed house. Cluskey, an Irishman who came to New York in 1827, is thought to have trained with the architectural house of Town and Davis. From 1830 to 1847, while living in Savannah, he designed several homes and public buildings in Georgia. He designed the Hermitage Plantation house in 1830, the Medical College in Augusta between 1834 and 1837, the main building at Oglethorpe University in Baldwin County between 1837 and 1840, and the building for which he is best known, the Governors' Mansion in Milledgeville between 1837 and 1839. It's interesting to note that Cluskey designed the Sorrel House during the same period that he designed the above, and after that, he continued to design large, Greek revival-style houses for Savannah's wealthy elite. He is credited with designing the

Champion-McAlpin-Fowlkes House and the Philbrick-Eastman House. He was appointed city surveyor in 1845, and in 1847 he moved to Washington, D.C. where he offered plans to renovate public buildings including the White House and the capitol, but nothing came of those proposals, and he returned to Georgia in 1869 where he began work on the lighthouse at St. Simons Island that had been damaged in the Civil War. He contracted malaria in 1871 and died at the age of 63 before the work on the building was completed. He leaves a large body of impressive works in Georgia. Francis Sorrel's ability to retain and afford someone of his reputation is indicative of his connections and wealth.

Conclusion

What makes the life of Francis Sorrel worth documenting? Jeff Freymann, his great, great grandson and his wife Ruth in their paper "The Greatest Generation," explain best.

> *"In that one man's lifetime, the fabled Deep South, that land of beautiful women, gallant men and stately mansions (which for a very few, really did exist) bloomed, blossomed, and died."* (p. 29)

The Sorrels' are interesting not just for their individual stories, but because their lives represent and parallel a whole way of life that prospered, died a violent death, and was laboriously rebuilt through reconstruction and change.

Francis Sorrel was indeed a survivor, just as his father had been, and much more so than his wives and several of his children. He took whatever life dealt him and reinvented himself to adapt to the situation at hand. He began life as a privileged child, lived to overcome abandonment and hardship, fought his way back to privilege, survived the Civil War with his fortune and most of his family intact, and died not long after the Antebellum South he loved ceased to exist. Though one might not admire his principles or approve his methods, one can't help but admire his tenacity and perseverance. His life and the lives of his wives and children allow an inside look at the most conflicted period of American history, and though the view from a modern day perspective may be at times unsavory, it is no less important or interesting to look upon. Those of us allowed the personal glimpse of the past owe a debt of gratitude to those who have preserved the opportunity. I, for one, am grateful.

Made in the USA
Lexington, KY
06 March 2018